Marcy Blesy

The Secret of Silver Beach

By: Marcy Blesy

Cover design by Cormar Covers

Chapter 1

"What's on tap today, Meg?" Brian asks as he sits up in bed, rubbing his eyes.

I watch him reach his arms up in what can only be described as a sexy stretch, but I have more important things to do than stare at my fiancé as he gets out of bed. "I'm interviewing a child about her fundraising idea to raise money for childhood cancers. She's making custom-colored bracelets to sell through her online Etsy store. She's the number one storefront in her genre. It's really quite amazing."

"Sounds cool."

"And there's the typical holiday-related stories, of course."

"Are on-air costumes in your future, my little princess?" Brian asks as he jumps back into bed and plants a kiss on my forehead.

I push him off playfully. "Unfortunately, I'm learning all sorts of things about the differences in reporting news at a major Chicago news station versus hosting a midday show."

"Co-hosting," Brian smiles.

I throw a pillow at him and walk to the bathroom. "I'd like to forget about that part."

Trenton Dealy. I thought Brian was cocky when I first met him at WDOU, but compared to working with Trenton, the early days of work with Brian were like being with an overly excited—but sweet—puppy.

"Be tough, Meg. Don't give him the satisfaction of seeing you upset. You've had practice dealing with arrogance," Brian winks at me. "I'm going to shower at the gym. See you tonight. Have a great day." He kisses me on the cheek, grabs an apple, and heads out the door of his condo. Soon we will condo hunt for our own place, and I can't wait for the day when we aren't living out of duffle bags as we move back and forth between Brian's downtown condo and my apartment in the Chicago suburbs.

I still take the "L" train to the studio like I used to do when I worked at WDOU. I wouldn't say that I'm afraid, but ever since I was assaulted and robbed earlier in the year, I'm definitely more aware of my surroundings. I wear a small cross-body purse that I grip tightly and a whistle around my neck. I don't like living like a fearful animal, but PTSD is real; so the more prepared I can be, the easier it is for me to travel on the train. And even though the four teenagers who attacked me have all been arrested and taken plea deals putting them in prison for years, I still can't help but wonder if their friends are out there and waiting to attack again.

"Hi, Meg," says Becca as I slide into the chair for my hair and makeup, which is a much bigger deal for a co-hosting job than for a reporter. There are perks to this job.

"Hey, Becca. Sorry I didn't have time to stop for coffee this morning."

"No worries. I'll drink the station coffee," she laughs.

"I hope you don't choke on the coffee grounds."

"I'll be sure to sue the company if I do."

Her smile lights up the room, and I'm reminded that there *are* good people that work with me at Chicago Midday. Tom followed me from WDOU, too, so having my favorite camera operator on the other side of the camera every day is another positive benefit, although I think he misses running with a camera on his shoulder or at his side. Standing behind a stationary camera is a new skill. Plus, I think he's put on a few pounds from not getting all those extra steps running around the city. I certainly won't be the one to tell him that, though.

"Have you seen the call sheet for the Halloween show on Friday?" Becca asks.

"Not yet. Trenton and I have a meeting with Char today. It must be bad if hair and makeup got advance notice." I raise an eyebrow in question.

Becca nods her head. "Oh, it's most definitely going to be a busy hair and makeup day." She grins evilly and puts a finger to her mouth. "But I will let Char break the news to you."

I roll my eyes and take a deep breath. I remind myself that I took this job because it gives me more latitude to dive into stories that are most important to me such as my hospice story and my bucket list story at WDOU. I am not limited by minutes-long time constraints for storytelling at Chicago Midday. I can go in depth and ask the questions that I want to ask. But the trade-off is having to do silly things such as eat unusual foods or learn hip hop dance moves or wear Halloween costumes *on camera* and live in front of thousands of people.

"All done," says Becca.

I look in the mirror one last time before heading to my meeting with Char. My eyes shine much too brightly for the morning hours, but I can't deny that Becca and her techniques make me look prettier and more sophisticated than my thirty years of age. My shoulder-length brown hair hangs straight today but shines with health and no frizz. Becca is a miracle worker.

"Thanks, Becca. I'll bring you a mocha tomorrow morning as long as you're still here—you know, assuming that you don't choke on those coffee grounds from the coffee maker today."

"I can only hope for the best. Have a great day, Meg!"

"Someone needs a watch," I hear when I walk into Char's office.

"Good morning to you, too, Trenton," I say through gritted teeth.

"Hair and makeup are taking longer and longer every day, Meg. Perhaps you should help Becca out and do some moisturizing of your face and eyebrow plucking *before* you come to work. That would likely save her a lot of time."

"Really?"

"I'm serious. I'm only looking out for you, Meg." He smiles, his giant eyes nearly popping off his face. But I can't deny that those eyes translate well on a television screen.

"Play nice, kids," says Char as she walks into the room and takes a seat behind her large black desk. Char's purple stripe in her black hair matches her office chair.

"Meg knows I am only teasing." Trenton flashes a quick smile in my direction.

"It's a big week," says Char.

"That might be an understatement," I say to the producer of Chicago Midday.

"Although everything is a *first* this year, we anticipate that our Halloween show on Friday will bring big ratings. People will tune in just to see the costumes that the two of you are wearing. Plus, we've got holiday cooking segments and decoration making and new music from Alaban. Busy, busy, busy!" She smiles through her stress. She thrives off the chaos of producing a new midday show in a large viewing market. Char flips her chin-length hair behind her ears and puts on her reading glasses. "Meg, I need you to meet with Danni about the cooking segment for today's show. She will walk you through what you will be doing. Trenton, there's a police officer coming in to discuss a new neighborhood watch program in the city. I've sent you an email about talking points."

"Char," I say, interrupting, "Who's the officer? I had a lot of contacts when I worked at WDOU. Maybe I could take that story."

Trenton starts waving his arms wildly in the air. "Hold on a minute here. Meg doesn't get all the feel-good stories just because she's a girl. I can handle the police officer."

I glare at him. "First of all, I'm a *woman*, not a *girl*. Secondly, it's not a feel-good story. It's an important story about limiting crime in the city through the help of its citizens. And I was just saying that…"

"Just because *you've* been a crime victim doesn't mean you should get all of the crime stories. Damn, Meg. You are really going to milk your assault for as long as you can, aren't you?"

I ball my fingers into a fist. I have never wanted to hit someone as much as I want to hit Trenton Dealy right now.

"Stop it, you two. I told you to play nice. I've given you your assignments. When you are done with them, you both need to meet sometime today with Clive. He's going to fit you for your costumes on Friday. I am not kidding, though." She looks from Trenton to me with a stern look on her face. "If you two don't improve your attitude with each other, this show is going to fail, and then we are all out of jobs. The audience can sense chemistry, and yours is sorely lacking, especially here. Pretty soon you won't be able to hide it on air if you don't work on your relationship *off the air*. That is why...." She takes a deep breath. "That is why I have signed you up for an escape room."

"What the hell is that?" Trenton asks before I can.

"It's a room with puzzles and activities you have to solve together. You have a time limit, so in order to *win* the game you have to work with each other within a set amount of time."

"You can't be serious?" I ask. It may be the first time Trenton and I have agreed on anything since we began working at Chicago Midday a month ago.

"I am very serious. I worked hard to get this program approved. It was years in the making. You were each chosen for your unique skill sets. I'll be damned if I will let you two prove me wrong because your egos are too big to coexist, so if you need practice working together productively, then practice you will get. You are scheduled to be at this address tonight at 5:30 p.m. Don't be late and *don't* fail this challenge."

Char reaches across the desk and hands me a piece of paper with an address on Lyndale Street in Bucktown with the name *Ed's Escape Rooms* written on it. I look up at Trenton, seething inside because the only one with an ego problem here is him, but he's already turned his back on us and stomped out the door.

Texting Brian in between segments and appointments with staff today is the only thing that is getting me through this day. Acting in minor roles in my high school's plays did not serve me well in bluffing my way into a pleasant on-air performance with Trenton.

Tom pulls me aside after my cooking segment with Chef Abby from the Golden Finch Café. Danni and I had made frosted layered cakes with various-sized eyeballs sticking out the sides. Who would want to go through so much trouble baking a cake that would most likely be demolished within minutes by unappreciative kids? It went fine, though, I guess, until Trenton came over for a taste test and stuck his fingers in the frosting to get a laugh from the audience.

"Meg, what's wrong with you today?" Tom whispers.

I raise an eyebrow and nod my head in Trenton's direction. "Char's making Trenton and me do some stupid escape room game tonight to force us into working together. We will fail. The writing's on the wall."

"Well, you *will* fail with that attitude. Meg, don't give Trenton the satisfaction he wants. He loves riling you up. He's not as bad as he acts—*all* the time, at least. Danni and Becca were just raving about how he'd sent them coffee last week from the new shop down the street."

"Huh. I didn't get coffee. Anyway, you sound like Brian."

"I seem to recall you didn't care for Brian when he started at WDOU, either. Now look at you two lovebirds." His eyes twinkle in merriment.

I sigh. "I know you are right—that you are *both* right—but Trenton has no soul. Brian has a soul. He was trying to find his place, to prove himself. Trenton doesn't have anything to prove. He's been in Chicago at WEDY for over ten years. He left the station at the top of his game to come here. The city is in love with him. Heaven knows why, but the audience loves him."

"You intimidate him." Tom says it so quietly I barely hear him.

I nearly spit out my iced tea.

"It's true. The audience also loves *you.* He's been a solo anchor for a long time. Did you ever think that maybe he was so successful and loved by the audience *because* he was a solo anchor? Maybe he does better alone. Maybe there's a reason he was alone at the anchor desk."

"Well, if there *is* a reason, don't you think they'd have known that before they offered him the job? He left a pretty cush position to come to Chicago Midday to have a job that came with a co-host."

"You were a relative unknown, at least compared to Trenton. No offense. I don't think he gave it much thought that he'd have to work so hard to share the limelight with someone else that is also popular—and getting more popular by the day, I might add." Tom smiles. "I've seen the ratings."

"Thanks, Tom. I appreciate the pep talk. I've got to meet with Clive about my costume changes for Friday's

Halloween show. Tell Anita hello for me. Oh, and take that hideous Halloween cake home with you. She'll get a good chuckle."

Chapter 2

I stop at Brian's condo after work before heading to *Ed's Escape Room.* I still can't believe that Char sprung this little excursion on Trenton and me with such little notice. I suppose that was the point; no time to make a believable excuse. Brian's still at work. He is happily living the life of the 6:00 and 10:00 news anchor which means we are like two ships passing in the night, barely seeing each other except for weekends and quick moments in the early morning and late-night hours. It works for now though wedding planning has definitely suffered. There is so much to do, and yet we haven't even set a date.

I change into a pair of jeans and an oversized Chicago Cubs sweatshirt. I throw my hair up in a ponytail and change into my comfy Sketchers. I want nothing more than this night to be over, but Tom and Brian are right that if Char went to the trouble to set this up then we'd better find a way to get along or—as she said—all of our jobs are on the line.

I call an Uber to take me to Lyndale Street. I'm so anxious for tonight that I don't need to add the further worry about having to wait around for a train later—with the possibility of something bad happening again on the train platform. And to hell with what Trenton said. I am not milking anything. I wish I could forget the whole thing ever happened and that those kids had never violated my sense of security. But it happened. And I *can't* forget it. Thank goodness there'd been no trial. All four teens took a plea deal: three years in prison. Adult prison. It hadn't been my idea to treat them as adults, but the city prosecutors are trying to make an example out of gang members who commit crimes as teenagers, trying to scare them into behaving, I guess. It doesn't feel good knowing they are locked up with grown men who have committed terrible crimes, but it feels good knowing they are not walking the streets waiting to terrorize other unsuspecting people like me who are just minding their own business and trying to catch a train home after a long day at work. I'd told the judge that in my victim impact statement.

Trenton stands up when I walk into the lobby of *Ed's Escape Room.*

"Don't start," I say, putting up a hand to stop him from complaining that I'm late. "My Uber got stuck behind a stalled car. Let's just do this and be done, okay?"

"Uh-huh," he says, frowning. "I already got the directions. There's a monster coming to destroy the city.

Blah. Blah. Blah. We have to figure out the one person who can stop him by solving a bunch of puzzles. If we don't figure out the right person, the monster comes and everyone in the city dies. And we lose. Got it?"

"Uh, okay, I guess. What are the puzzles like?"

"I have no idea. The employee said we'd figure it out once we're locked in the room."

"Locked in?"

"I don't like the idea of being locked in a room with you any more than you want to be locked in a room with me. But we have this walkie-talkie. We get three clues if we need help, and we have one hour."

"Fine. Let's start then." I follow Trenton down a long hallway to a black door marked *Danger*. A woman appears and quietly opens the door for us. I can hear it click shut behind us once we are inside.

I start trying to decipher an "ancient" hieroglyphic puzzle while Brian turns objects over in the room. "What are you doing?"

"The lady said we have to consider everything in the room a part of the puzzle."

"Well, you're making a huge mess."

"And you're making zero progress! Switch with me then." Trenton pushes past me so that he is standing in front of the puzzle.

"I almost have the puzzle figured out!" I shout as my voice echoes off the walls.

"You're taking too long! Go read that note tacked to that dummy's jacket," he says, pointing to a stuffed doll that is sitting on a chair pushed up to a table with a full place setting in front of it.

"No. *You* read the note yourself. I am going to finish this puzzle."

"You are being a real bitch, you know," he says as he huffs off to the dummy.

I can suck it up on camera. I can play nice if I must, but nobody gets away with calling me a bitch. I whip my head away from the puzzle so that I am facing Trenton. "Do not call me a bitch ever again."

Trenton scoffs. "Here!" He throws the doll at me. "The note says to use his shoes to press into a shoeprint mold somewhere in the room. Maybe that puzzle you're failing tells us where to find the mold."

I close my eyes and count to five before returning to the puzzle. Each of the images corresponds to a letter. I move them around until they spell something that makes sense. "Under bookshelf three," I say aloud. "Look under bookshelf three."

Trenton looks for numbers on the bookshelves. "Here it is. Number three." He moves the bookshelf back and forth until it pivots forward displaying a mold that looks like it was made for shoeprints.

I stand the doll up in the mold so that its shoes fit perfectly. A red light turns on. "Now what?"

"How am I supposed to know?" he asks irritably.

"Use the walkie-talkie," I say, signaling to the radio in his hands. "Get a clue."

"Are you serious?" He shakes his head back and forth like I'm the crazy one. "There's a green light on top of that table in the corner. I imagine we have to make it light up, too."

"And there's a blue light on top of that coat rack," I say, pointing to the rack that holds various-sized hats instead of coats. "Maybe the hats have clues." I glance at the clock. "We are halfway through our time and haven't made a lot of progress. Let's get a clue."

"No way, Meg. I am not a cheater."

"It's not cheating. She literally told us we could get three clues. Do you want Char to be angry that we failed this challenge? Stuff your pride back in your pants and ask for the clue. In fact, just let me do it!" I reach for the walkie talkie, but Trenton sees me coming. He pulls his arm back as I reach forward, and the momentum of my forward reach sends me sprawling to the ground. I know what's happened the minute I hit the floor because I've made impact with the dummy doll's chair first—with my mouth. I sit up and spit blood into my hand. And a tooth. A front tooth.

Trenton's eyes are like saucers. "What did you do?"

I don't answer, but I can't stop the tears from falling down my face.

Trenton grabs the dummy's napkin from his place setting and holds it out to me. I take it, grateful to wipe away the blood that is spilling out of my mouth.

Trenton pushes the button on the walkie talkie. "We need to be let out. My co-worker made a stup—*fell*—and she needs medical attention. Quickly, please."

Trenton pats me on the head like I'm a puppy. It's the nicest thing he's ever done for me.

Chapter 3

The manager gives me a bag of ice before I leave. She looks ticked that she has blood all over the floor and some of her props. She keeps mumbling about losing money because she'll have to sanitize the room before it can be used again. I watch Trenton write something down and give it to the manager before we walk out the door—maybe the show's contact information because *I'm* sure not paying for this debacle. I apologize profusely. I really do feel bad about ruining her night, but I also need to leave because I am bleeding like crazy and need to get to a dentist quickly.

Trenton holds the door open for me as we leave. I pull out my phone to call for a car.

"Put that away. I'll drive you wherever you need to go. Just try not to get blood in my car." He smiles slightly.

I'm too emotional to know if he's being an ass or teasing. We don't talk in the car though I've managed to call my dentist.

"See you later, Meg," is all Trenton says when he drops me in front of the emergency clinic my dentist directed me to. What a disastrous night!

I punch Brian's number into my phone before walking into the emergency dental clinic. Surprisingly, Brian picks up his phone, but when I look at the clock, I realize I've caught him in between the 6:00 and 10:00 news. I can't talk, though, partly because of the blood pooling in my mouth and partly because I can't stop crying now that I'm alone.

"Meg, what's the matter? Are you hurt? I can't understand you." His voice is full of concern.

"Trenton wouldn't take a clue and wouldn't give me the walkie talkie and I reached for it and I fell and I hit the du and my tooth fell..."

"Meg, stop! Slow down. I don't understand anything you are saying. Did you say you lost a tooth?"

Through my tears, I manage to convey what happened, at least the part about Trenton being a jerk and me tripping because of him and losing my tooth and so...much...blood.

"Take a deep breath. It's going to be okay. I promise. Meg, tell me you know that."

I shake my head yes, but of course Brian can't see me.

"Meg?"

"I promise."

"Have you called the dentist?"

"Yes. He's at his son's little league baseball game. He told me to go to an emergency clinic near Garfield Park. Trenton just dropped me off."

"Good. Call me when you're done. I love you."

"I love you, too."

I'm late to hair and makeup because I spent most of my morning staring in the mirror and practicing talking without opening my mouth wide. The dentist wasn't able to save my tooth even though I'd brought it with me. It was cracked down the center. He'd said he'd never seen a tooth do that before. Lucky me. I'll get an implant to replace the broken tooth, but that is a multi-month process, so the next step will be a temporary bridge with a fake tooth. However, through another stroke of luck, he was short-staffed at 8:00 last night, so I'd come home with a hole in my mouth and an appointment later today for a temporary bridge.

"You can do this," Brian had said. *"You have to go to work. Don't give Trenton the satisfaction he wants. And he did drive you to a dentist. That's something, Meg."* His pep talk didn't match well with his desire last night to drive to Trenton's

fancy high-rise condo he was always bragging about to beat the crap out of him.

Becca's eyes say it all first. "What happened to you?"

I fight back tears again as I slump into the chair. "Is it as bad as it looks to me?" I ask, opening my mouth slightly.

"Oh, yes. It's bad. I mean, sorry. But you have a hole in the front of your mouth."

"Just today. I'm getting a temporary tooth tonight. It's all Trenton's fault."

"Did he…did he hit you?" She says it so quietly I can barely make out the question.

I laugh. I shouldn't laugh, but I do. "No. I tripped in an escape room and knocked my tooth out, but I tripped because Trenton wouldn't give me something I wanted, so…"

"So, it's his fault?"

"Do you doubt me?" I'd never considered that anyone would think this was *my* fault.

"No way. I mean, he didn't *push* you, right? But I can totally see him annoying you enough that you'd stumble and..."

"Stop." I raise my hand in the air. "I understand how this looks. You're right. I tripped on my own, but he..."

Becca puts her hand on my arm. "Meg, I understand. It's Char that might need convincing, though." She points to my boss who is walking toward us with a quicker succession of steps as she gets closer.

"Hi, Char," says Becca as she pauses the foundation application on my face.

"Hello, Becca. Meg, I need to see you in my office in twenty minutes. Is that possible for you, Becca?"

"Of course. She'll be as ready as she can b...she'll be beautiful."

Char nods and walks away.

"Does that mean she knows?" I whisper when Char is gone.

"Well, you smiled with your mouth closed, so she didn't *see* your holey mouth," Becca giggles. "I'm sorry. It's so cute. Plus, you have a kind of whistle when you talk."

"Not helpful."

Becca shrugs her shoulders and finishes applying my makeup and combing out my hair, leaving it straight to pull over my face if needed.

Char is not alone in her office. For two days in a row, I get to be lectured with Trenton sitting next to me. That is not a good start to the new gig.

"Sit down." She doesn't waste any time. "Trenton tells me you had an accident last night that prevented you from finishing your team building challenge. I'd like an explanation—that I'll believe." She looks at Trenton.

"Char, I already told you what happened. I think Meg was a little tipsy at the start of the game—I can't be sure—and tripped over her own feet. Knocked herself out flat and caused a giant mess. There was nothing I could do." A giant smile creeps across his face.

Char turns to look at me. Surely, she can read my face as I know my eyeballs are nearly popping out of my head.

"Kidding! Just a joke, Char." Trenton sits back in his chair and waits for me to say something.

I take a deep breath before speaking and saying something I'll regret. "I didn't drink before meeting

Trenton. We had a…disagreement over when to use the walkie talkie to ask for a clue. I lost my footing when I reached for it from his hands."

Char's mouth drops open. "Did you knock out a tooth?" She stands up and walks toward me.

"I…uh…yes, but tonight I will have a temporary tooth put in before getting an implant in a few months. Today is the only day like this, and I thought maybe if Tom pulled the camera back that no one would…"

"Are you kidding me? Everyone will notice. *Everyone.* You two are ridiculous. You're worse than toddlers." She throws up her hands in exasperation.

"You're wrong about this, Char," says Trenton. "I had nothing to do with Meg's clumsiness." He looks at me and shakes his head like a disappointed parent.

"If you think I believe your crap, Trenton, you're wrong."

"But I…"

"Shut it," she snaps. "Meg, who is your dentist?"

"I don't know. I mean, I know who *my* dentist is, but I went to an emergency dentist last night."

"Give me his number. We need to get him on the show today." Char picks up her phone in anticipation of the phone number.

"Excuse me?" I ask because I really am confused.

"We'll use it."

"It?"

"We'll use your fall to make you appear silly and cute and charming and highlight Chicago's fine emergency dentists. The audience will eat it up," says Char, her eyes dancing in delight at her perceived brilliant idea.

"Only *you* could make your idiocrasy into a ratings boost," says Trenton as he hangs his head and walks out of Char's office. "Only you," he mumbles again under his breath.

I can't believe I'm sitting live in front of thousands of Chicagoans with a giant hole in the middle of my mouth. Not only am I sitting on camera, but I am sitting here with a *closeup* camera shot of my face. Dr. Ainsley is quite delightful on camera, I must admit. Trenton is doing most of the questioning while I sit here like a trick pony opening my mouth wider every time they discuss a new technique or information about emergency dentistry. I can't wait for this day to be over.

When Dr. Ainsley has left the studio, Trenton corners me in the lobby. "You might have won the battle today, Meg, but you will not win the war."

"I don't even know what war you are talking about. Why do we even *have* to be at war? Why can't we get along—for ratings at least?"

"Because I was supposed to be the headliner for Chicago Midday until you started gaining notoriety after your 'train station attack,'" he put in air quotes. "And then the bigwigs decided a co-hosted show featuring the *talented, beautiful, blah, blah, blah* Meg Popkin would be a better idea. I didn't agree then, and I certainly don't agree now. You're bringing down this show with your insistence that we cover emotional stories. This is supposed to be a pop culture, flavor-of-the-city kind of show. Your very presence is changing the essence of this show. And it sucks. The show. And you. You know, I actually felt a little bad for you last night until you decided to use this whole situation for your own selfish motives."

Trenton turns to walk away, but I won't let him. I block his path. "You can have whatever opinion of me that you want to have, but I was brought onto this show for a reason, and it's not because of my assault at the train station. I am a good reporter. I care about people. And there is an audience for the kinds of stories I want to tell about people. If *you* can't share the spotlight because of your egotistical, narcissistic personality, then you will continue to live a miserable life; but I, for one, love this job and love this show, and I refuse to let you ruin it." I push past Trenton and back into the studio, not stopping to take a breath until I am safely back in my dressing room.

During the next segment, I embrace my mouth issues. Danni is making sweet potatoes with miniature marshmallows. I take a marshmallow and place it in my mouth where I'd lost my tooth. The studio audience roars with laughter. Danni sticks a marshmallow over her front tooth, too. Tom takes a split screen shot of the carved jack-o'-lantern on set and me. I'm sure the picture will go viral on Chicago Midday's social media. At least I lost a tooth during a holiday week when oddities are celebrated.

Chapter 4

A glass of wine awaits when I walk through the door at 3:00 p.m. I'm still not used to the hours of my day—starting super early but ending in the middle of the afternoon.

"What are *you* doing here?" I ask as Brian clanks his water glass to my wine glass.

"That's a nice greeting," he says with the dopey dimple grin that first attracted me to him at WDOU.

"Sorry." I kiss his cheek. "But I don't usually see you until after the late news. Is everything okay?"

"I told Jerry I needed to slip away for a meeting. I thought you might need a friendly face, my jack o' lantern bandit." He grabs me by the waist and kisses me full on the mouth.

I knew from the moment I accepted Brian's marriage proposal that I'd never regret it. "You could not be more correct."

"How's the mouth?"

My eyes fill with tears. I don't mean to cry. I don't like to cry, but ever since Dad died, any talk of pain or concern or stress sends the tears falling. "My mouth really hurts." I look like a helpless toddler standing there in

Brian's kitchen with tears falling down my cheeks and a pouty look on my face, except for the wine glass, of course.

Brian takes the glass and sets it on the counter. "It's all going to be okay," he says. "Work *and* your mouth." He pulls me in for a hug, and I let him hold me until my heartbeat matches his.

"Thanks for doing this. It means a lot."

"I wish we had more time." He winks at me.

I roll my eyes. "I suppose you're wishing to add being with a toothless freak as a notch on your bedpost?"

"Something like that," he grins. "But I need to get going. Call Lara, though. She's texted me like ten times trying to find you. You really need to stop avoiding her."

I sigh. I'm not trying to avoid my older sister's texts. It's just that I know what she wants. She needs help going through Dad's things, and I'm avoiding it. Blue Lake Hub, the condo where Dad lived in Blue Lake, Michigan's Cooperative Community, is pressuring us to clear the condo. There's a waiting list to get in, for obvious reasons now that we know the secret of Blue Lake, that people think that the waterfalls in town give longevity to its residents who have been diagnosed with terminal ailments. And even though Dad ultimately met the fate of his illness and the waterfalls held no special powers, he'd sworn that the peace and joy and friendships he'd experienced there in the last months of his life were worth every bit of time spent away from Lara and her family and me in Chicago. While part of me selfishly wishes Dad had never moved to Michigan, the more rational and empathetic part of my brain *and* heart knows that he did exactly what he had to do and needed to do to come to terms with his diagnosis. And there is certainly no denying that Dad found the peace he was looking for. But there are people wanting that condo, especially since Dad had the top floor with the best view of the lake. The condo board had been more than generous to give us this extra time to clear out Dad's condo though we'd paid for it financially.

"Okay, I'll call her this afternoon."

"Good girl." Brian kisses the top of my head.

"Thanks again. Do you have a busy night at work?"

"Not too bad. A little fraud, a little car accident, a little drunk and disorderly—nothing too unusual." He laughs.

"Don't forget to sprinkle in some good news, too."

"That's Ariel's job."

"Then I know she'll do a good job. She's so much more sincere in her delivery than Jessalyn ever was."

"Well, when you are named after a mermaid, can you help yourself?"

With a final kiss goodbye, Brian walks out of the condo, leaving me to my half glass of wine and a nagging avoidance of my sister that can't be ignored any further.

I grab a blanket from the back of the couch and take it and my wine to Brian's balcony. Something about the nonstop noise of the commotion on the busy Chicago streets below gives me comfort. I pull out my phone to call Lara.

"Well, look who has reemerged to the land of the living," she says before a simple *hello.*

"In my defense, if you caught the show today, you'd have seen why I was a little preoccupied."

"The tooth thing?" she asks with irritation.

"Yes, I guess you can call it the *tooth thing.*"

"Look, I'm sure that was really painful and all, but I need your help, Meg. The condo board keeps calling. They are threatening to take all of Dad's things and throw them out in a week if we don't come get them. The boys have full schedules this weekend. Rick is swamped at work. I simply cannot get to Blue Lake this weekend. Life is too…"

"Stop, Lara. It's fine. Brian and I are free this weekend. We will go to Blue Lake."

"Really?"

"Really."

"Thank goodness. I don't think it will take you too long. We already did the big paring down of Mom and Dad's things before he moved, but you and I both know Dad couldn't let everything go. Did you ever see his closet there—floor to ceiling boxes? Still, I think you guys can move quickly. Pack everything up, and I will help you go through the boxes here. I promise. Plus, I'll split the cost of the moving truck with you."

"Lara, slow down. You don't have to split anything. Dad's trust will pay for a moving truck. Plus, we only need the truck to take donated items to the thrift store in town, right? You don't want any of the furniture, do you?"

"No."

"That money from the trust is for just this type of thing as we are closing out Dad's affairs."

"Closing out." Lara pauses for a moment.

"Yeah, it sucks."

"Yes, it really does."

I hear screaming in the background followed by Lara's new overly enthusiastic puppy barking.

"I have to go, Meg. The boys are home from school, and chaos has ensued."

"Give them hugs from Aunty Meg."

"I will. And—thank you. I know this isn't easy for you, either."

Chapter 5

Becca is beaming when she sees me on Friday morning. "You made it on time—and *early,* no less!" she teases.

I hand Becca a Witch's Hat Frappe. "It's a big day, I hear. Something about a holiday and lots of costume, hair, and makeup changes."

"Ohh! Thanks for the drink."

"You're welcome."

Becca is wearing cat ears with a cat tail pinned to the back of her jeans. If only my costume could be so simple. Though I had my tooth fixed yesterday with a temporary crown until I can have my tooth implant put in, Char and Clive thought it would be hilarious for my first costume appearance to be *without* my tooth again, so Clive has figured out a way to make me look like I am still missing a front tooth. Becca pulls my hair back in a tight bun.

"That should work," she says, admiring her work. "A helmet will fit nicely over your head."

"Fabulous," I say sarcastically. "I'll be back for the next change."

Clive is waiting for me in the clothing department. "Meg, darling, you need to be prompt today. Lots to do. Lots to do!"

He hands me an oversized Chicago Blackhawks hockey jersey with the name *Popkin* on the back. It's hard to imagine that won't be my name for much longer. Then he hands me a helmet and a fake mouthpiece that makes it look like I am still missing a tooth. I place the helmet on my head, but Becca's bun presses so tightly against the back of my head, that the front of the helmet is askew.

"Oh no, no, no. We can't have that. We have to see your mouth. We have to see your *tooth*."

"You mean my no tooth placed over my fake tooth because I lost my real tooth?" I smile largely showing Clive my *fake* tooth.

He grabs the helmet, which is still on my head, and roughly readjusts it to his liking so that my mouth can still be seen. This is going to be a long day. Trenton walks into the room, and Clive hands him a jersey with his last name *Dealy*. He pops it over his head and puts on his helmet. Somehow, even with a helmet on his head, Trenton's hair likely remains unmoved.

"Thirty seconds to go time!" we hear Tom yelling from the studio.

I follow Trenton toward the set. "Still trying to overshadow me?" he whispers.

"What are you talking about?" I whisper back. "We are literally wearing the same costume."

"Yeah, but you'll get the laughs because of your tooth escapade. Still capitalizing on your mistakes. Typical."

"Take that back," I spit.

"Five, four, three, two…"

I squint my eyes one last time at Trenton and take a deep breath before turning to the camera. Knowing that my friend Tom is standing on the other side of the camera helps. "Welcome to Chicago Midday on our first annual Halloween special episode," I say. "Boy, do we have some treats for you today!"

"Yes, we do, Meg," says Trenton, smiling at me. "First up, we have Connor Lucas of our very own Chicago Blackhawks joining us to talk about his charity work with the Juvenile Diabetes Research Foundation."

The interview is predictable and on brand. Connor Lucas praises me for committing to the costume though he and the rest of the audience don't know yet that my fake tooth has been applied.

After the interview, I race back to Becca's chair while Trenton meets Clive for a costume change. It is so not fair that men don't have to worry about hair and makeup in the same way women do. It's such a double standard. "Nice job, Meg. Next up, Daphne!" Becca throws a red wig over my hair and applies fake eyelashes. "Beautiful! Scoot over to Clive for your purple dress. And don't forget to have fun!"

Trenton is walking out of his dressing room when I pass him in the hall. He's wearing a white shirt, blue pants, and an orange neck ascot, along with a blonde wig, perfectly placed by Clive. *Fred* to my *Daphne.* Barf.

As Fred and Daphne, we are joined on set by Danni as Velma, Clive—who'd spent a week growing a scraggly goatee— as Shaggy, and Becca in a giant Scooby Doo costume. Even Tom got in on the festivities by dressing as a criminal in a Creeper mask behind the camera. Of course, the banter leads to my miraculous tooth improvement as I let the audience in on the fake missing tooth bit from the first segment. Trenton is quiet while Shaggy and Velma chatter away. We introduce the Chicago band Alaban after airing a cooking segment featuring caramel apples with Danni and a local confectioner. Danni had insisted on feeding Trenton caramel apples which he tried to rebuff, and she'd left me alone, I presume, due to my precarious tooth situation.

While Alaban is singing, Becca orders Trenton and me into the two chairs at her station. Clive applies dark eye shadow on my eyelids while Becca applies a whole pallet of color to Trenton's face. I have to give it to the woman. She is very talented. And while she's working, she babbles on with Trenton who could not be any sweeter. Then Clive and Becca switch places. Clive puts a crazy white wig on Trenton's head, while I get my own hair combed out, teased, tied up in a high ponytail. I rush to my dressing room to put on a formal red dress while Trenton changes into a black and white striped suit in his dressing room. I have to admit we look damn good when we see each other for the first time in the hallway: Lydia and Beetlejuice.

"You can't say I'm stealing the show now," I say. "You look just like Michael Keaton."

"Well, you *do not* look like Winona Ryder, at least 1980s Winona."

I follow behind him as I stomp onto set. We are bombarded with a hundred kids visiting from the Boys and Girls Club of Chicago's Southside branch. They parade in their own costumes throughout the audience who pass out candy provided by Char and the team at Chicago Midday. The joy expressed on the faces of the kids and the volunteers reminds me why I took this job. Trenton is not raining on this parade today.

And when I get back to my dressing room, I grab my phone. I shouldn't do it, but I can't help it. I click through to my voicemails. I find the one dated August 21 and push the button.

Hey, Meg. Wanted to tell you how proud I am of you. You're going places in this world. Anyway, it's Dad in case you didn't know. Love you.

I stare at myself in the mirror as Beetlejuice's almost bride looks back at me with tears staining her face with black mascara.

Chapter 6

I drive the first leg of our trip to Blue Lake. Brian doesn't usually get home until after 11:00 p.m. and dragging him out of bed at 8:00 this morning had been a challenge, but I'd promised him it would be worth his while to get up early. He'd thought I'd meant sex when I made him my proposal, but I'd meant a last kayak ride across the lake. Something tells me he will receive the benefits of both opportunities.

I'd wanted an early start to beat the Chicago traffic that takes people to their second homes along the coast in Michigan, and I'd promised my sister that we'd hand over the keys to the Blue Hub condo board by Sunday afternoon. They have a cleaning crew ready to turn the condo over to a new owner on Monday. I can't help but wonder about the new owner and what ailment will bring him or her here to live out the last healthy weeks, months, years of life. While some people truly do get better in Blue Lake—and I assume that's why most people come—it's hope that sustains many of them until it just doesn't work anymore, their bodies fail, and they prepare for the next step in life, whatever their belief system may be. I'm grateful the board didn't force us to go through Dad's things when he was in hospice care back in Chicago. They'd been more than forgiving with the timeline. We have to get this condo emptied.

"Why didn't you wake me up?" asks Brian, stretching as I pull into the parking garage of Blue Lake Hub, three hours after we'd left with no stops for food, gas, or bathroom breaks.

"Your snoring was cute, so I couldn't wake you. Plus, I didn't have any coffee yet, so I didn't need an emergency stop."

"Wow, you must be super crabby without your coffee this late in the morning!" He moves out of the way before I can slug him.

"I do need a stop at Rosie's before we get to work. Not only do I need caffeine, but I also need food."

"Hangry?" Brian raises an eyebrow.

"If you don't want to know the answer to that question, you'd best keep your mouth shut. Come on."

I park the car, and we walk the few blocks to Rosie's Restaurant. Brian and I had prepared for our visit. We know the drill by now. Residents identify themselves with some sort of red-colored clothing or item. Visitors wear blue though they usually don't ever suspect why their loved ones thrust a blue jacket or blue-brimmed hat or blue bracelet at them. I run my fingers over the blue bracelet Dad had given me on one of my visits, the letter *M* dangling against my wrist. Brian and I had been too clever and persistent and reporter-like in our quest for the truth. Today we are each sporting blue jackets. No one will slip up and reveal the secret of Blue Lake that they all strive to keep so private lest they be inundated with people and media trying to sour their hope. *Blue means don't talk about the secret.*

The restaurant is as crowded as the first day Dad took us there. We wait a few minutes before a table opens. A couple with red jackets walks past us with a woman about my age with a blue vest. I wonder if she knows why her family is here. The board had lessened their rules a bit after Brian and I went to such lengths to sneak onto Hope Street to discover the waterfalls that so many here think can heal them, though they don't, of course. According to the man at Dad's funeral, some family members, as needed, are allowed to know the secret belief of this community. That makes me happy and proud of Dad for fighting for that allowance as so many people like Lara and me didn't understand why Dad would up and move his life so far away from his family.

"Hi, Meg. Would you like pancakes again?"

A young woman with a handkerchief on her head stands next to my chair smiling.

"Millie?" I ask.

"You remember me, too."

"Of course I do. I'd remember that smile anywhere. This is my fiancé Brian."

"Hello, Brian." She extends a hand to him though her wrist is shaking.

"Are you here to get your dad's things?"

"We are. He…" I take a deep breath. "He really loved it here, Millie. Thanks for being a part of his story."

"Is there anything you'd like me to tell him?"

I wrinkle my brow in confusion. "Excuse me?" I ask. Brian stares at her, wide-eyed, too.

"I'll be passing along soon, you know? This is my last week of work. I'm going home to rest—back to Arkansas with my parents. They are happy to know I am coming back."

"Millie," I say as I take her hand in my mine. "I'm so sorry to hear that you are leaving."

"Don't be, Meg. Blue Lake has saved my life, as silly as that may seem to *you,* and you do have some notoriety around here, Meg," she bends down to whisper. "People know who you are and what you did. Some people were really angry cause they thought you'd tell our secrets, especially cause you're on the news and all. But you didn't. And people respect you now."

I look around. There are several people stealing glances at our table, but I'd never have thought anything of it before Millie said something.

"Anyway, what shall I tell your dad when I get to where I'm getting? Cause I think he will be wanting to hear about you."

I glance at Brian. He nods his head. "Well, tell him that I'm engaged now—to Brian. And that, uh, that…that I miss him terribly, that Lara and I do. But most of all, tell him I'm really happy he's at peace and that he found comfort the last few months of his life in Blue Lake."

"Sure thing. And I will be right out with those pancakes, too." Millie turns to walk away and back to the kitchen.

"Was that weird, or is it just me?" Brian asks when Millie is out of earshot.

"Weird. So weird."

The brain has a way of remembering that is so powerful it can nearly knock your socks off—and that's what happens when I walk into his condo. The smells—the smells hit me first. Dad's aftershave permeates throughout the condo, faint yet present, as if wrapping me in a hug in every room I enter. I don't cry. I'm nearly cried out over Dad, but my heart is heavy.

Brian understands. He feels it, too, even though he knew Dad for such a short time. "Do you want to sit out on the balcony for awhile before we start going through things?"

I shake my head. "No, we have a lot to do and not much time to do it in." I put my hand on Brian's arm. "But thanks for the offer. And thanks for being here."

"There's nowhere else I'd rather be. Plus, this is where I first knew."

"Knew what?"

"That I was going to marry you." He takes my hand and pulls me toward his body. "And I've never looked back—only forward."

I let him hold me for a minute, inhaling his strength for what we are about to do. "I love you."

"I know," he says quietly.

We start packing in the kitchen. It seems like the most straightforward room. Lara and I had decided that anything we packed up should be given to the local thrift store in town. Dad had loved thrifting, and to think that others might find joy in his things like he found joy in theirs is comforting. Plus, Lara and I took anything sentimental we wanted when we helped Dad pare down for his move to Michigan—pictures of him and Mom, his high school ring, Mom's quilts, old yearbooks. There can't be much here that we will take with us except for personal items. The moving truck we rented for a few hours tomorrow was probably a silly rental, but it will make it easier to bring things to the thrift store. They know we are coming, and they seem pleased.

"Why did your dad bring so many glasses with him?" Brian points to a variety of assorted glasses and mugs that spread out over three different shelves in a tall cabinet.

"I have no idea. Trust me. Lara and I tried to get him to limit what he took when he moved, but he did what he wanted to. He always did." I take a deep breath and reach for a mug with this saying: *It is not in the stars to hold our destiny but in ourselves.* "Well, I understand why he kept this one," I say, holding the mug up to Brian.

"Yep, that was Paul, deciding how *he* wanted to live his life."

"And how he wanted to die."

We double our efforts as we box up blankets in the living room, books and more books in the guest room, various knick-knacks that hold no meaning for me. It's not until we get to the bedroom that I decide we need a break. "Ready for that kayak ride?" I ask, wiping sweat from my forehead on this particularly warm November day.

"You bet, but no tandem rides for me. I want a real race." He smiles so widely I think his cheeks might pop. I'm a lucky girl.

"After the theft of the tandem the last time we were here, I don't think that will be a problem."

We walk toward the lake hand in hand with our blue t-shirts on full display as no jackets are needed now. There is a steady stream of people milling about. I recognize some of the faces, but most I do not. Such is the circle of life—in and out, in and out. It's so sad, but I know for the residents here, they are mostly happy and content with their plight in life.

The *Ken's Kayaks* sign has been changed. It now says *Kristin's Kayaks.* I wonder at the same time what might have happened to Ken and if your name has to start with a *K* if you're going to run a kayak stand in Blue Lake.

"Good afternoon," says the woman who looks to be about my age. "Looks like two singles are in order for you." She smiles and points toward the dock. When she does, I see the bruises on the inside of her arm, another reminder of the cruelties of life. I wonder what her condition might be.

"Thank you." I want to smile back, but I am too sad to make the effort.

"Everything okay, Meg?" Brian paddles his kayak alongside mine in the middle of the lake.

"I'm just thinking about how much sadder Blue Lake seems now that I know everyone here is dying."

"Yeah, it was easier to get charmed by the infectious joy of the people when you didn't know the *why* of why they were here. But, if they can find the joy, we have to see the joy they've found. Nobody lives forever."

I sigh. "But it's not fair."

"Nope. So, I think we should focus on living our lives with as much fun as we can because we don't know how many of those days we are promised."

"Well, I *did* show my hillbilly mouth on national television this week."

"And don't forget that sexy red wig."

I splash Brian with my paddle. "If only I could find the joy with that ass of a co-worker I have."

"Trenton is a topic I won't allow you to discuss this weekend. We are focusing on *fun.* Ready, set, *go!*" Brian splashes his paddle back and forth as a fury of water splashes into my boat, but I'm ready for the challenge. If there's one thing I know, it's that a good old-fashioned competition can improve my mood.

We pick up sandwiches at a food truck between the library and Hope Street. That's a new addition to Blue Lake. It will be a long night of going through the things in Dad's room where most of his personal belongings remain. There's no time for a restaurant tonight.

"Do you think Tweedle Dee and Tweedle Dum still work on Hope Street now that some of the family members are allowed to be in on the secret of the waterfalls?" Brian asks as we walk past the entrance to the magical healing street of waters that gives neither magic *nor* healing.

"They are still there," I say, pointing to two large men who appear busy sweeping up the street but with watchful eyes in every direction.

"Should we say hello?" Brian laughs.

"Oh, hell no. They'd probably send me to waterfall jail the way we fooled them."

"Ha! That's my girl. Love to see that smile. Come on. Let's get this done."

We link arms as we walk back to Blue Lake Hub for one last time.

Chapter 7

The boxes Lara spoke about are piled floor to ceiling in the back of Dad's walk-in closet. There are five of them. The first ones I take out have some of Dad's favorite books. I recognize the titles: *To Kill a Mockingbird, Animal Farm, The Bible.* They are unremarkable to some, but to me they are a part of my father. He loved learning. He loved stories. And if I hadn't become a journalist, I'd have become a librarian. That love of books came from Dad.

"This box has a bunch of papers," Brian says, setting the box on Dad's bed. "Do you want to go through it with Lara in Illinois?"

"No, she's so busy with the boys, and we are fine on time. I think I'd like to take a look now." I rifle through the papers and find many I recognize: Mom and Dad's marriage certificate, Dad's college diploma from the University of Illinois, a copy of my birth certificate along with Lara's, notices for the births of Lara and Rick's kids, an old bill of sale for Dad's 1985 Chevrolet Cavalier.

Brian grabs a stack of papers to thumb through before passing them off to me. "This guy kept some pretty cool stuff. His collection is top notch. I mean, look at this ad for a Harley-Davidson motorcycle from 1975!" Brian holds up a piece of paper pulled from a newspaper.

"Let me see that! There is no way my grandparents would have let my dad get a motorcycle!"

Brian hands me the newspaper pull out ad. I see the ad, but it's what is on the back, written in ink, that catches my attention. *Johnny L, Stevensville, Michigan* with a phone number. "I wonder why Dad saved this." I point to the message.

"Meg, think about it. How many thousands of post-it notes with names and numbers do you have in your office right now? It could literally mean *anything.*"

"True. Maybe it stands out to me because we passed an exit for Stevensville on our way to Blue Lake." I set the newspaper ad aside and continue going through the box. I find more of the same: pictures of Lara, Mom, and me from our many vacations, Florida, Maine, Tennessee. I try to hide a particularly embarrassing picture of me in overalls at the Grand Canyon, but Brian grabs it out of my hand.

"Look at that sexy thang!" He rolls over to his side on the bed as he laughs. "You were really working those UGGs, too."

I sigh loudly. "Overalls *and* UGGs. Why didn't my mother stop this disaster?"

"Cause her style choice wasn't much better!" He points to my mom who is next to me in the picture. She is wearing a neon green track suit.

"I know they say that style trends recycle, but I can't imagine these looks ever making a reappearance. And I am pretty sure Mom's style was already outdated by the time this photo was taken."

Brian flips through the next papers in his box. He pauses as he stops to read. "I didn't know your dad was adopted," he says, holding up an official looking piece of paper.

I snatch the paper out of his hands. "He wasn't adopted. What are you talking about?" I read the same thing Brian had read. It's a birth certificate. At the top is the name *Paul Lamont* with the date of birth December 23, 1960—Dad's birthdate. The parents are listed as Sarah Jackson and Gordan Lamont.

"What's the city of birth?" Brian asks, trying to read over my shoulder.

"It says St. Joseph, Michigan."

"Is that anywhere near Blue Lake? I don't know a whole lot about the geography of Michigan. When I was growing up, my family didn't travel north very often from Arizona."

"An hour or two, I think. I went there once when I was in college. I was visiting my roommate. It's a cute little beach town although a lot of those towns kind of blend together in my mind. Is there anything else in there?" I point to Brian's box as I ponder what I am looking at. Grandma and Grandpa Popkin had been some of my most favorite people in the world when I was growing up. They'd lived in Door County in Wisconsin on a beautiful piece of property in the country, overlooking the rolling hills of the peninsula on the other side of Lake Michigan from northern Michigan. Dad had been an only child, and they'd doted on him with the love you'd expect to be laid upon an only child. Grandpa had been a fruit farmer. Dad had learned the value of hard work from him though I imagine he'd been disappointed when his son left Door County for college and never returned, except to visit, only to move to the metropolitan Chicago area. They'd died when I was only 14, both of them, within a month of each other. Grandpa died first followed by Grandma. Dad had said she'd died of a broken heart. I'd believed it then, and I still do now.

"Everything else looks normal," says Brian who is thumbing through the papers in the box. "Are you planning what I think you are planning?" Brian asks.

"What do you mean?"

"Are you going to hunt these people down, or at least their families, as they may not be alive?"

I shrug my shoulders. "Part of me says to leave the past in the past. Whatever those papers mean doesn't change anything. Dad was raised by a great family."

Brian doesn't say anything but gives me a knowing look as he raises his eyebrows.

"Stop it! I can leave this alone."

"Uh-huh. Just like you could leave Hope Street alone, right?"

"I'm a reporter. It's in my blood."

"And that's why I love you. Whatever you decide is fine with me. Plus, your adventures are always fun, if not a bit illegal or naughty, too."

He leans in for a kiss, and we fall back onto the bed. It's too weird being in Dad's old room to be intimate, so instead I settle into the crook of Brian's arm and let him hold me as I try to process all the questions that are running a marathon through my mind.

The next morning, after we'd made our stop at the thrift store with Dad's things, I scan the condo one last time before closing the door and walking away from a very odd, yet uniquely special part of my father's life. I hand the keys into the Blue Hub office, knowing that they will have a cleaning crew upstairs within the hour to prepare for the next resident. I wonder about the journey his or her family will embark upon soon, what questions they will have, and what outcome will result.

"Are you okay?" Brian grabs my hand as we walk to my car in the parking garage.

"I'm fine. To new adventures, right?" I tenderly touch my engagement ring.

"Onward and upward."

Chapter 8

Char called Trenton and me back to her office before our first segment, an interview with local actor Heather Galek about her new role in Chicago Paramedics. Trenton arrives before I do, so I take a seat next to him to await whatever Char has to say. Neither of us speaks, Trenton scrolling through his phone and me staring out the high-rise office window wondering what Char could possibly want to tell us now.

We don't have to wait for long as Char starts talking the minute her foot crosses the threshold into her office. "I could not be more disappointed in the two of you," she says.

"Char, you don't…"

She raises her hand in the air. "Shut it, Trenton. Despite the exceptional holiday ratings—thanks in part to Meg's tooth debacle earlier in the week—the chemistry between the two of you is blowing up and *not* in a good way. Social media is killing us. Everyone sees it. Look at this." She pulls out her cellphone and holds it up, expecting Trenton and me to read from her screen.

Meg and Trenton set the stage on fire…as their hatred for each other simmers below the surface.

Even NFL hockey players have more love than Meg and Trenton.

"Ouch," I say.

"Damn straight. And this is only a tiny sampling of what's out there. You are like two toddlers fighting for attention from their parents. Well, if I'm to be your parent, I can tell you that the games, the power grab—whatever it is you are doing—*has* to stop. I've worked too hard to get this show approved. If you can't work on your relationship, then one or both of you will be replaced. Do you understand me?"

Char's voice raises to a level I have never heard before; and I don't like it, especially since I don't think I've done anything to receive her wrath. Neither of us says a word, our heads locked forward staring past her.

"Good. I assume you hear me. So, today, after work, the two of you will go into the conference room and hash it out—whatever your differences are. Get them out. Yell and accuse, whatever you have to do, and then leave it in the room. This is your last opportunity." She leaves the office before either of us has a chance to complain.

I walk straight to hair and makeup. Becca listens with an empathetic ear, but I can tell she agrees with Char.

Trenton and I have to figure this out like adults. We can't continue working together with such visceral loathing. I don't think he's able to change, and I don't think I need to, either.

I watch Trenton interview Heather Galek. He's sickeningly sweet the way he interviews her, yet underneath the surface of his questions is an air of condescension. Heather doesn't seem to notice, likely too overjoyed to be receiving attention for her new role on such a big show, but I can sense it. I can't respect someone like that, so I don't know how our meeting in the conference room is going to change anything. I wish my dad were here. He always had the best advice.

Clive hands me an apron with turkeys on it before I walk on set for a cooking segment with Danni about Thanksgiving preparations. It shouldn't be shocking that we've moved on so quickly from Halloween to Thanksgiving, but it is. Can't we breathe before our rush to the next holiday? Americans are always in such a hurry. They forget to live the in-betweens. That's something Dad taught me—to appreciate the time you have to live now. Perhaps that's the advice I need to get through this meeting with Trenton, even if I must swallow my pride.

After changing into jeans and a navy blue pullover sweater, I tug my hair into a high ponytail, refill my coffee cup at the Keurig machine in the staff room—a recent upgrade—and take a walk to the conference room. It's only at the end of the hall from the staff room, but it feels like I am walking five miles, each step weighing heavier and heavier.

Trenton enters the room after me. He throws a yellow legal pad on the table and sits in the head chair. That figures. I resist the temptation to sit at the other end of the table, and, instead, take a seat next to him on the adjoining side of the table.

"This meeting is stupid. You know it, and I know it," Trenton begins, "but you have to make changes, or you're going to tank this program."

"*We* need to make changes, or *we are* going to tank this program," I correct him.

"Take a piece of paper and write down your grievances." He pushes the pad of paper at me. "I'll do the same. Then we'll read them. You make the changes, and we can get the hell out of here. I have a hot date tonight for an early dinner, and I am not going to let you screw that up!"

I take a slow breath and hold in what I really want to say. Instead, I rip off the top sheet of the paper and begin to write my frustrations and concerns.

You cannot accept sharing the spotlight with me.

You blame every failure or perceived failure on me.

You are condescending and chauvinistic.

You have no respect for my abilities.

There is no reason to act jealous.

I stop writing because I think I've summarized my thoughts well. When Trenton sets down his pen, he slides his paper across the table to me. I do the same with my paper. We read silently.

Meg…

You ask stupid questions nobody cares about.

You ask too many questions.

You don't let me get my time with the guests.

You butter up to Char and Becca and Clive and Tom and Danni and everyone else here so that they don't like me as well.

You let Clive dress you in too many bright colors.

The last one makes me laugh out loud which only pisses Trenton off. I have to try *something,* though, or one of us is going to be fired. "Look, Trenton, I ask the guests the questions you perceive that nobody cares about because part of our audience *does* care. We aren't a hard-hitting news show. You like the entertainment part. I like the Chicagoland community service part. We should each rise to our strengths instead of cutting each other down or judging each other's work."

Trenton nods his head, likely having come to the same conclusion that we have to at least *try* to agree on something. "You're right. I'm much stronger with the entertainment news. Maybe we should propose to Char that instead of doing all the segments together, we each get a few segments to ourselves."

"I like that idea. Yes, that's a great solution." I speak too sweetly for what I'm really feeling inside, but I know what works with people like Trenton. I haven't gotten to where I am in this industry without reading how to handle people, even if I've been failing terribly up to this point with Trenton. "And I can keep my colorful wardrobe contained to my segments." I try to say that out loud without laughing, and I don't intend to let *anyone* tell me how I can dress, except maybe for Clive. He is an expert, after all.

"That would be good, Meg. I mean, seriously—you wore a yellow and white striped skirt on national television today."

I contain my comeback reminding Trenton that we are a local show and not national, but I don't say anything. "Go have fun on your hot date. I'll tell Char our idea about separate segment hosting."

"No way. I'm going with you. Knowing you, you'll try to steal my thunder and make her think it was *your* idea and not mine."

"Better yet, *you* tell Char yourself. I'm going to catch a train out to my sister's place for dinner. See you tomorrow, Trenton."

"Yep," is all he says as I walk back to my office for my jacket. What an ass.

Chapter 9

Nolan, Owen, and Blake attack me the minute I walk into my sister's house with cries of "Aunt Meg! Aunty Meg!" Truthfully, it warms my heart. Now that both of their grandparents are gone on their mom's side of the family, I am all they have left for extended family on the Popkin side—and Brian—as being an uncle is something he's already had practice being with his niece in Arizona.

"Boys, for goodness' sake, leave your aunt alone. She's a famous star now. We don't want to hurt her."

She winks at me. I know she's proud. She's a bit dramatic sometimes, but she is a good big sister. Just then the new puppy, Scooter, runs into the room and pees at my feet. He's black and white and adorable, all wrapped into a tiny ball of energy. And he can hold a lot of pee for such a small dog.

"Why did I agree to let these boys have a dog? Blake, take Scooter to the backyard, please. Owen, get Mommy the carpet cleaner. Nolan, no! Do not touch that pee!"

After Lara has cleaned the carpet and shooed all of the kids *and* the dog into the backyard, she collapses on the couch.

"Are you crying, Lara?" She wipes her face with the back of her hands.

"No, I'm not…it's just…it's just a lot."

I put my hand on Lara's knee. "I think you're doing a great job. You're managing a zoo here, you know?"

She laughs. "I suppose so. Thanks. So, what did you want to talk about?" she asks as she hands me a glass of iced tea—extra ice—something Mom and I both enjoyed together.

"I wasn't going to tell you, but I knew I would want to know if you knew so…anyway, here." I thrust Dad's birth certificate into the hands of my sister.

She reads through the facts, her eyes getting wider the further she reads. "But Grandma and Grandpa Popkin?" she asks, staring at me.

"I know. It doesn't make sense to me, either."

"Grandpa and Dad had nearly identical curves in their noses. I never suspected. Do you think Dad knew? I mean, obviously he had this birth certificate, but *how long* did he know? And why didn't he ever say anything?"

"I have no idea." Neither of us talk for a moment.

"Are you going to look into it?"

"Should I?" I was hoping this would be Lara's reaction. For some reason I felt like I needed her approval before I went digging into our family tree. I certainly had caused enough trouble looking into Blue Lake when Dad moved there.

"It won't change anything, right?" She grips the birth certificate. "We are still Julie and Paul Popkin's children. It was *Dad's* life that changed, not ours, so…I think…I think if you want to look into these Sarah and Gordan people, you should." Lara hands the paper back to me and takes a long drink of her iced tea.

"Okay. I'll start with a Google search."

"And tell me what you find out. You don't have to be afraid to tell me whatever you find, okay?"

"Okay."

"Promise?"

"I promise."

She glances toward the boys who are still playing outside with Scooter before blurting out. "I think Rick is having an affair." Her hand is trembling as she holds her glass.

My eyes widen in surprise. I shake my head back and forth. "No way, Lara. He adores you and the boys. Why would you suspect that?"

"Because he comes home late from work, and he's distant. He's too tired for… you know…sex. I can't believe…." She sets down her glass and gets up to move to the kitchen and out of the eyeline of the boys.

I follow her, gather her in a hug, and let her cry. "Lara, you have to talk to him."

"I've tried. He says he has a lot on his plate at work. He says nothing is wrong. He's just overworked and tired. Meg, I don't want to do life without Rick. He's my best friend. And the boys…." She chokes back another round of tears.

"Do you want Brian to talk to him?"

"No. I don't know. Maybe. What would that do?"

"Sometimes guys will talk to other guys about things they won't talk to their wives about."

"Okay. Thank you, but don't tell anyone else besides Brian. It's so humiliating."

"I won't say a word. Lara, look at me." I hold onto her arms until she is facing me. "It is all going to be okay. I promise."

All she can do is stare at me, neither of us confident if that's a promise that can be kept.

After playing with the boys and successfully sending marbles along a variety of twists and turns on a race to the bottom, I give hugs goodbye and walk to the train station to go back to Brookfield. I can't stop thinking about what Lara said. It doesn't seem believable that goofy, lovable Rick who'd been head-over-heals in love with my sister for nearly a decade could be unfaithful. But I have to set those thoughts aside for a moment as it's time to say goodbye to Linda.

Chapter 10

Linda and I have been through a lot together in the last three years. She'd been my first roommate at my apartment in Brookfield. She's been my confidante and cuddle buddy. For a cat, she cuddles more than most—if she likes you. Granted, there aren't many people that she likes, but she loves me. When I was mugged on the train platform, she'd tolerated Brian who'd insisted on sleeping here for several nights when I first came home from the hospital. But they hadn't bonded. Linda didn't like Brian stealing her cuddle buddy, and Brian didn't like testing his allergy shots by getting too close. Now that Brian and I are getting married, it's with much sadness that I have decided to give her up. I can't expect my fiancé to take allergy shots every month for the rest of his life just so I can keep her. And with my cat sitter neighbor moving to her own house this week, now is the right time to let her go. They have a special bond, and though I don't know if Linda will forgive me, I know that she will be loved and give love, too. Plus, my neighbor has promised that I can visit any time I'd like. She's moving to Minnesota, though, so I don't know whether that invitation will ever be redeemed.

When I get home, I lay on my bed. Linda knows the drill. She jumps onto the bed and onto my stomach, kneading over my midsection until she is comfortable enough to settle into a seated position. I wrap her tail through my fingers and pet under her chin. She purrs with glee. I don't realize I am crying until my nose gets stuffy. I wipe away the tears, but they come faster and faster. It's not just Linda I am crying for but Dad and Mom and changes that are happening so fast: the new job, the stress of the wedding planning that hasn't yet begun, Lara's concerns, the uncertainty of the future. Through all the tears, Linda has moved from my stomach to my chest. She butts her head against my chin, even stopping to lick my face as if I were one of the kittens she's never had.

"I know, Linda. It sucks. But life is still good. You have to see the good. There's lots of good to come." I'm not sure if I'm talking to her or to myself.

Chapter 11

Char smiles more than I have ever seen her smile on a Friday morning. She's obviously been pleased with the week and how Trenton and I have been *behaving*—her words, not mine. I think of it as more of an avoidance, but it's working. We haven't had one fight, even during the segments we still had to do together like the Midday Moments section at the beginning of the show where we go over current events. It had proven easy to divide up most of our assignments. I had taken stories such as the young boy who'd raised money biking over 100 miles through the suburbs to help his classmates afford a field trip to Six Flags. I'd interviewed Keri Hasky, the director of Neighborhood to Neighborhood in Naperville who was organizing a large food drive for the upcoming Thanksgiving holiday. Trenton had taken segments like interviewing local hip hop star Tony MkBony about his upcoming concert series at Wintrust Arena and showing off his stellar planking ability with a personal trainer from the largest gym in downtown Chicago.

Char knocks on my office door after I've returned from the set after taking off the fake eyelashes that Becca had insisted I try out. They make my eyes itch. "Come in,"

I call out. Having my own space to close the door is a definite improvement over my tiny public cubicle at WDOU.

"I wanted to stop by and tell you that your work is being noticed—in a good way—by management. And by me."

"Thanks, Char. Just doing my thing." Could I have sounded more stupid?

"Seriously, Meg. I want you to know that your hard work has never gone unnoticed. I know how difficult working with Trenton can be, but if anyone could figure out how to make it work, I knew you'd be the one. You don't take crap from anyone, but you know when to dodge the throws. You pick your fights wisely. And for that I am grateful. It makes my job much easier…and more enjoyable."

"Wow. Thanks, Char. I appreciate the kind words."

"I want you to know that is the truth. You are appreciated."

"I understand. Thanks again, Char."

She doesn't leave. Instead, she starts tapping on my doorframe. I realize she's never fully entered my office.

And her bright smile from this morning has disappeared. "But, well…there's no good way to say this."

I pull my glasses on as I'd also taken off my contacts when I took off my fake eyelashes, and Char has been blurry during this entire conversation. "What is it, Char?" I sit up a little straighter.

She sighs. "I've just finished a long meeting with management—virtually. Wouldn't it be nice if they actually came down to the show once in awhile?" She sighs. "Management wants more banter between the hosts. They *love* the work you've been doing, like I said."

"You've mentioned that a few times in the last ten minutes. What are you trying to say?"

"Meg, I'm…I'm only the messenger. I have argued on your behalf, but I don't hold the money strings here."

"Am I being fired?"

"Of course not!" Char yells so loudly she realizes that others in the common area are staring at her. She shuts the door and enters the office fully for the first time.

"Then spit it out…please." I am starting to sweat, and I wonder why I didn't reapply my deodorant.

"You're being reassigned. It's only temporary. Management wants to test some other hosts to see if they have better chemistry with Trenton."

I imagine my eyes must look like ping pong balls right now, but I cannot believe what I am hearing at this moment. "They want to test someone for better chemistry with *Trenton?* Why don't they test someone who will have better chemistry with *me?* You've been in here blowing up my ego with compliments. Was that supposed to soften the blow that I'm being demoted? Because—no disrespect, Char—but that's a shitty thing to do."

"I meant everything positive I said about you, both from my own feelings to those of management. The show was created for a two-host format, Meg. You have to understand that. And for whatever reason, Trenton is the co-host they want to test other hosts with. For what it's worth, you would have been my choice. But I'm not the final decision maker. I'm sorry. Truly. I am sorry."

"Now what? Do I pack up my office?" I am trying with all my strength to not start crying.

"We are asking you to travel, just for a little bit, until they figure everything out."

"Travel? What's that mean?"

"They want a story about offseason traveling up the coast of Lake Michigan, all the way around the lake."

I blink a few times to clear my mind. "You mean that you want to send me on a trip around Lake Michigan from Chicago to Wisconsin to the Upper Peninsula of Michigan to the lower peninsula, to Indiana, and back?"

"Yes, but the other direction. We want you to go to Indiana and the lower peninsula of Michigan first. And you won't be alone the whole time. Tom will join you for part of the trip, and—and some of the trip will be self-taped."

"Self-taped?" I rip the piece of paper I'd been holding in half in frustration.

Char wrinkles her forehead. "Just for a couple of weeks," she says softly.

"You do realize that Thanksgiving is coming up?"

"I know. I'm sorry, Meg. It's the best I have to offer until a few different co-hosts have come through. Then management will re-evaluate."

"Re-evaluate." I repeat the word as if it's foreign to me.

"It's the best I can offer right now. I'm sorry."

"Does anyone care that I left a good job at WDOU to come to this show? That I was scouted for this job?"

"Yes and yes. But so was Trenton. I'm confident they will see Trenton as the problem child, Meg. You only have to wait it out. Plus, you love Michigan and traveling. You told me how you were visiting recently, right?"

"To clean out my dead father's condo." I don't give a damn that my words drip with sarcasm. They exude my real feelings.

"Oh, I'm sorry. Look, I have to go now. I'll send you a file with possible towns to visit and story ideas. I'm sure you'll come up with other ideas, too. And every few days you'll do a live call in with the show to report on your discoveries in addition to providing videos. The audience won't know why you have this assignment. They'll just appreciate their favorite news person traveling around the lake. Think of yourself as the next Al Roker of the Today Show." She attempts a slight smile.

"He's a meteorologist."

"The file will be in your inbox in ten minutes. Check it out. And, Meg? Try to see this as an opportunity. You'll be great." Char shuts my office door.

As soon as she's gone, I plop my upper body onto my desk and exhale the breath I didn't realize I'd been holding in. "Opportunity, my ass," I say aloud.

Chapter 12

Becca, Clive, and Tom raise their drinks—beer for Tom and margaritas for Becca and Clive—in a toast to me at Hess House Brewery after work. No amount of lying could convince Becca that I was okay after my meeting with Char, so she'd rallied the troops for a little pick me up. I wanted to get home with Linda and snuggle on the couch and tell her all of my problems, but when I thought about her and that she didn't live at my apartment anymore, all I did was cry more.

"To Meg," says Tom. "To the hardest working, most dedicated host of Chicago Midday! May you thrive on your adventures around the lake and return to this pit of misfits to kick Trenton Dealy's ass to the curb!"

"Here! Here!" they all shout.

"Thanks, guys. I really appreciate what you are trying to do."

"I still can't believe they're doing this to you," says Becca. "Who are they going to find to test with Trenton? He's threatened by everyone he shares airtime with."

"Except for Dorothy the Dancing Dalmatian!" says Clive.

Everyone laughs.

"He wasn't threatened because that dog was terrified of Trenton. She hid behind her trainer until he stepped like five steps back," I say.

"I have to admit I got a tight shot of his face when she cowered. Classic."

"You should win an Emmy for the fine camera work," says Becca.

"Nah, maybe if I'd caught the dog peeing on his leg or something like that, but she waited until the stage was empty to pee on my camera pole. I watched the whole thing!"

"Are you serious?" I ask.

"Serious as a choir boy in church!" says Tom.

We all laugh again, and I take a long drink of my wine. Even if this job ends up being short-lived, it'd have been worth it to meet Clive and Becca and to spend more time with my work brother Tom.

I decide to stay with Brian in the city tonight. I didn't text him yet because he's at work, and I didn't want to worry him. There's nothing he can do about my new "opportunity" anyway. It's 8:30 when I park on the street to the side of his condo building—only on-street parking for guests. It's dark out this time of year. The air is cold as I pull my sweater tighter. I grab my jacket and toiletries bag from the backseat and assess my surroundings before getting out of the car. I wonder if I will ever be able to be out at night in Chicago by myself and not feel nervous or afraid. Being assaulted changed me. I think about the teens who are sitting in an adult prison right now because of the choice they made that night to steal my purse. All they had to do was ask, and I'd have given them money. But they didn't ask.

I'm sitting in Brian's living room watching old episodes of *House Hunters* when he gets home from work. I'd watched him on the 10:00 news. He is thriving in his new job as anchor at WDOU, and I am thrilled that at least *one* of us is fulfilled at work.

"Hey, sunshine! I didn't expect to see you tonight. You didn't text. Everything okay?"

I walk toward him and open my arms for a hug. He brings me in close. I inhale his light cologne, a mix of musky and familiar. I shut my eyes and pretend I am on a quiet beach away from all the troubles in the world.

Brian pulls away. "What's wrong, Meg? Look at me." He puts one finger under my chin and tips it up.

Once I've started talking, I don't stop until the end. Brian is quiet as I explain all about Char's surprise reassignment and proposed trip around Lake Michigan for a new travel segment.

"Well, that sounds like a crappy day," he says, taking my hand and leading me to the couch. He sits down next to me. "It's not going to work, you know?"

"What's not going to work?"

"They are not going to find anyone better than you to test well with Trenton. They will see that *he* is the one that has to go."

"Maybe, but what if they *do* find someone who can tolerate him and fawn at his feet…"

"…who can *also* be a good co-host and anchor? No way. It won't happen."

"I wish I could believe you."

"I have an idea. Here, hold out your hand."

I do as Brian says. He mimics putting something in my hand and then closes it.

"What are you doing" I ask.

"I am giving you some of my faith—in you and in this whole crazy situation—that everything is going to work out okay. You don't have enough faith yourself, so I'm sharing. And if I ever need it back someday, I'll know where to find it. It's something my mom taught me when I was little. Plus, you love to travel, and you're going to get a kickass trip around the greatest lake in the country."

"How did you turn out to be such a great guy?"

"Maybe I met a girl who saw through my rough edges and decided I was worth getting to know, and a little bit of her goodness rubbed off on me?"

I nod my head in agreement and snuggle into Brian's chest. Right now the world seems righted on its axis no matter how off course it really is.

Chapter 13

I call Lara on my way to work, my last day on the air in the studio before I begin my two-week trek around Lake Michigan. It's early, but I know she's up with the boys. Plus, Rick would have left for work. She was supposed to talk to him again last night.

"Hey," she says quietly when she answers the phone just before her voicemail comes on.

"Hi. Is this a good time to talk?"

"I guess." I hear the clank of dishes as if she is emptying the dishwasher.

"Did you talk to him?"

"Yes."

"What did Rick say?"

"He said I was being ridiculous."

"Is that all?" I ask, swerving to avoid a car that has moved into my lane. With my new job—which I feel like is becoming my *old job*—I often drive to work now. There's assigned parking, and a few more people than I'd like now know who I am. I don't want the hassle of having to be nice and answer questions or sign autographs at 7:00 in the morning. "Lara? Are you still there?" It's like pulling teeth getting her to talk.

"I'm still here."

"Did Rick say anything else?" I check the time on the dash—7:05 a.m. I'm late. What does it matter, though, really? What are they going to do—*fire me?*

"Yes," she says, slamming the dishwasher shut.

I try to remain calm, but my oldest sister is testing my patience. "What did he say, Lara?"

"He said he's been lying to me."

"But…but I don't understand. You said he denied an affair."

"He's not having an affair, Meg."

"Okay. That's good, right?" I pull into the parking garage and look for spot 821, Meg Popkin's parking assignment. I wonder if the test co-hosts will get assigned parking, too. Maybe they will get *my* parking spot.

"I guess." She sounds detached from this conversation which isn't unusual as there is usually a kid begging for her attention, but there is no little boy background noise today—or a puppy barking.

"Lara, I'm in the parking garage. I need to get to the studio. Is there anything else I should know?"

"Rick has a brain tumor." She says it so quietly I can barely hear her.

"Oh my God," I pray.

"He's been seeing doctors, not telling me." And then she bursts into tears—her heart leaping from repression to pouring forth in a jumbled string of unintelligible sentences and high-pitched wails.

"Lara…*Lara!* What did the doctor tell him?"

"Rick has a brain tumor! Didn't you hear anything I said?"

I text Char a quick message to let her know I am in the building but dealing with a family emergency. "I heard you. I can't imagine how scary that must be. But medicine is awesome, and Rick is young and healthy."

"I'm going with him to the doctor today. Can you watch the boys?"

I'm caught off guard as Lara rarely asks me to babysit—something about my lack of experience with kids and letting them walk all over me. I always thought that's what aunts were *supposed* to do—spoil their nephews. I have a thousand things to do to prepare for my travel tour, as Char has been calling my trip around the lake, but how can I say *no*? "I'll be there at 3:30, okay?"

"Okay," she sniffles. "Thanks." Then she clicks off the phone.

Before rushing up to the studio to be beautified by Becca and Clive and having to fake it through one last taping with Trenton, I ponder whether knowing your husband was having an affair would be better than knowing he had a brain tumor. What an awful choice.

I feel like a zombie walking absently through my last day in the studio, at least for a while. I admit that it helps me to be less annoyed by Trenton's play at niceties when I am reminded again of the fragility of life and what matters the most.

"We are *really* going to miss your cheerful face every day around here," Trenton says as we sign off after a day of low-key interviews that included musical guest B. Ivers who had taken down the house with her rendition of Aretha Franklin's *Respect* after singing her new single.

I smile too sweetly. "Thank you so much, Trenton, but I want to remind the viewers that you will still get to see me every day with my Lake Michigan travel adventures."

"Oh, of course, Meg. We can't wait for your segments." He turns back to the camera. "Thanks again, Chicagoland, for joining us on another week of Chicago Midday. Tune in on Monday to see our new guest co-host."

I wait until Tom shuts down the camera before removing my microphone and getting up from my seat on the couch. I turn to walk away.

"Not even so much as a *goodbye* from the great Meg Popkin?"

"Why would I say *goodbye* if I'm coming back?" I don't wait for an answer as I walk away.

Tom and I finalize plans with Char in a quick meeting at the end of the day, so I can get to Lara's house to watch the boys. Tom is way more excited about this assignment than I am. He's thrilled because the company has decided to give him a stipend that he can use any way he'd like in addition to his regular salary. He plans on using the money to have Anita join him for much of the trip. They never had kids, and they are the cutest couple ever. If Tom is my big brother, Anita is like an older, wiser cousin. I could use some sage wisdom on this trip.

"So, are you clear on your mission?" Char asks for what seems like the tenth time we've gone over our itinerary for this trip.

"Showcase off-season and fall happenings in the many small towns around Lake Michigan that are all within driving distance of our viewership, whether they start the trip toward Wisconsin or Indiana with Michigan in the middle either direction they'd go. Visit the places identified already that know we are coming to tape but talk to the locals who might give us more information or stories. Sell the experience. Blah. Blah. Blah." I have no more energy or cares to give.

Chapter 14

The boys jump on me the minute I walk in the door. Blake has just gotten home from school, so he's begging for a snack. Owen is trying to play a trick on me by asking, *Aunt Meg, what's on your shirt?* and when I look down, he swipes his finger up my chin. I fall for it every time. Nolan is trying to fight for more attention than his brothers by hanging on my leg as I try to walk into the kitchen where Lara and Rick are talking quietly. And in the middle of the mayhem is Scooter who is licking my socks.

"Hi, Meg." Lara hugs me a bit too tightly, but I understand.

"Hi, Lara. Hey, Rick." I'm not sure how to act. How do you treat someone who's been like a big brother to you after they've been told they have a brain tumor? I understand more and more why Dad kept his diagnosis a secret from us for so long.

"No sour faces allowed!" he says, grabbing me for a big bear hug. "I need to see *someone* who can smile around here." He gestures toward Lara. "Low with this one power of positivity is," he says, trying to make his wife laugh as he winks at her.

"No sour faces I have," I say in response. "I've got things under control here. You can go ahead and leave."

Lara nods her head though I don't for a second believe that I have things under control, nor does my sister.

The minute Lara and Rick leave, Blake pulls me to the side, leaving his brothers to set up a massive display of their Matchbox cars.

"Aunt Meg, can I ask you a question?" He whispers so low that I can barely hear him.

"Sure, Blake. What's up?"

He glances at his brothers to make sure they are not listening. "What's wrong with Mom and Dad?"

My heart sinks. "What do you mean?" I am running old parenting stories through my head right now to recall whether lying to children is encouraged or frowned upon.

"They are whispering a lot. And I saw Mom crying in her bedroom when she didn't know I saw her. You can tell me. I can take it. I'm almost a man."

I resist the desire to smile—the innocence of preteens shining through in my wise nephew. "Sometimes adulting is hard, Blake. But everything is going to be okay." I add the last two words without thinking. "I promise." And I wonder if I've just permanently damaged the first one who made me an aunt by promising something that might not come true. How would he ever trust me again? And how would he ever survive without his daddy?

But he seems satisfied with my answer and returns to his brothers. For the next half hour, we line up cars by color, then by size, then by our ideas on which would be fastest in a NASCAR or Formula 1 race depending upon the type of car.

I put a frozen pizza in the oven while the boys build forts in the living room. I assume their parents don't let them use the blankets from the linen closet because they squeal with excitement when I say *yes*, but I pretend I don't know that rule. When Lara and Rick get home, we are eating pizza on the living room floor under a pile of hanging blankets and rearranged furniture. The boys try to *hide* by not making any noise, but Blake is too cool for school, so he climbs out first which angers his brothers who think he's spoiling their *best hiding place ever.* It reminds me of when he was little, and he'd hide in plain view in a game of hide and seek. I'd walk right past Blake pretending not to see him. Oh, to be that innocent again and not be burdened with the hardships of life.

Lara walks me out while Rick climbs into the tent with the boys. She holds a hand over her heart, trying to steady her breathing I imagine. "Rick needs surgery," she says as soon as we are out of earshot of the boys.

"Okay, that's okay, right?"

"No, it's not okay, Meg. My husband has to have brain surgery! *Brain surgery.*"

"But they will remove the tumor, and then he can go back to normal. Right?"

"If it's not cancer!" she screams, quickly covering her mouth. "Oh, Meg, I can't lose Rick. I just can't!"

She collapses forward. I catch her and hold her in my arms until there are no more tears left to cry. Sometimes there are no perfect words to speak. I hope she knows how much she is loved even without the perfect words.

"Thanks for watching the boys." She wipes at her face to hide the dried tears on her cheeks. Her efforts won't hide reality from her oldest son.

"You need to talk to Blake."

She snaps her head up and stares at me in confusion. "Why?"

"He knows something is wrong. He told me he's seen you crying."

"You didn't tell him about his dad, did you?"

"Of course not. Look, I'm not a parent, so I may not be the best one to give advice, but I know he's older now. He might need…"

"You're right. We will talk to him tonight, but we won't make it scary—just the surgery part. Okay, Meg? Please don't give him all the facts. We are trying desperately to keep them innocent for as long as we can. Dad's death hit him particularly hard."

"I won't say a word, Lara. You and Rick are amazing parents. You are going to get through this. And I'll be here for you—for all of you."

Lara nods her head. "Thanks, Meg. Now I have to go put my living room back in order!" She returns inside the house, and part of my heart goes with her.

Chapter 15

Brian has planned a special night for us before I begin my trek around the lake. He'd taken a rare day off from work, at least from the 10:00 taping of the local news. My bags are packed and piled in his entryway, awaiting my send-off tomorrow morning. Tom is taking the Midday van while I am driving my own car—gas refunded Char'd said. Oh joy—like that makes up for this miserable situation. Not having to plan for who will take care of Linda while I am gone does relieve some pressure, but it also makes me miss her even more. It's times like this that I wish I had a dog to keep me company on this adventure. Dogs travel better than cats.

I am sitting in the living room watching the 'L' train pass by below Brian's massive floor-to-ceiling windows when I hear the door open.

"Hey, babe!" I hear, perhaps a bit too chipper.

"Hi."

"Aww, you look so sad. Come here and give me a hug." Brian holds out a beautiful bouquet of multi-colored carnations.

"Those are really pretty," I say as I take the flowers and set them on the kitchen counter before coming in for a hug. "But I can't take them with me, you know? They wouldn't last in a car very well."

"True, but I will see them here and think of you. They will remind me of the wild sex we had the night before you left for your trip." He throws his head back in laughter.

I roll my eyes. "Oh, really? Is *that* what you think is going to happen?"

"No. That is what I *know* is going to happen."

Then he scoops me up and carries me into the bedroom. And I let him. Because being with Brian is exactly what my brain needs to shut off and be carried away to ecstasy. His touches are tender, but I need more tonight, and I give him the wild sex memories that he needs to remember me by while I am gone. When we are done, I collapse onto his bed and fall asleep. It's the most perfect peace to be wrapped up in the arms of the one you love and who loves you back.

When I wake up the next morning at 6:00 a.m., Brian is not in bed. I pull on a pair of Brian's boxers and my sweatshirt from yesterday and pedal into the kitchen. The smells alert me before I get there. "You made me breakfast?"

"Don't act so surprised." He flips a pancake with a spatula and checks on the sausage. "I need my woman well-fed. She has a big job to do."

I laugh, but it comes out more like a snort. "The breakfast is an amazing idea. The *big job* part is a joke, I'm afraid."

Brian turns off the stove. He wipes his hands on a towel that is hanging out of an open drawer. "I know this is a frustrating situation to be in. I get why you are angry. No one deserves that host job more than you. Trenton is an ass. But you have a great couple of weeks ahead of you. Do you know how jealous I am that you get to leisurely travel around Lake Michigan seeing the sites and meeting so many cool people? You *love* intimate storytelling, and you are *good* at it. You will shine through on your on-air segments. I know it sucks, but is there any part of you that can embrace the positives of this experience?" He grabs the spatula that is within reach on the counter, presumably so I don't smack him with it.

I don't say anything for a moment, collecting my thoughts. "You sound like Dad."

"Well, he was a very wise man—and handsome," he adds.

I smile. "Yeah, he was." I take a long, deep breath. "I'm sorry."

"You don't need to apologize." He squeezes my hand. "It's been a crazy year. You're allowed all the feels. But then use them to kick ass on this assignment."

I nod my head yes, smile at Brian, and dig into a piping hot plate of pancakes and sausage.

After showering, I dress in tan khakis with a white long sleeve shirt and a black cardigan. My first assignment is in Michigan City, Indiana, where I will be visiting Monroe Zoo. I have a feeling I won't need fancy shoes for much of this trip.

"Call or text me when you get to the zoo," says Brian as he kisses the top of my head while I am yet again buried in his chest. "I have some errands to run today. I might go out to see Rick later. I figure he could use a break from Lara." He shoots me a quick look. "No offense. I adore your sister, but she doesn't exactly handle stressful situations calmly, and Rick might need a more positive distraction."

"I think that's both an accurate read of my sister and a really sweet thing to do. Plus, the boys will be all over you. They exhausted me yesterday."

"Where are you headed after your Michigan City taping? Into Michigan, right?"

"Yep. I'm taping at Warren Dunes tomorrow, so the show is putting me up in a rental in a little town called Bridgman. I remember passing it on our way to Blue Lake."

"A rental? Fancy!"

"Nothing but the best for their star host," I say sarcastically.

"That's the optimistic spirit I knew was buried inside!" A large grin of merriment spreads across Brian's face.

"You're hilarious. You'll join me next weekend in Mackinac Island, right?"

"Yep. Oh, I forgot to tell you that I took that Monday off, so we'll have three days together."

"The great Brian Welter took an *entire* day off? For me?" I feel like bursting into tears, but I don't want to mess up my makeup.

Brian tips up my chin so that we are staring at each other. "I love you, Meg. I'd do anything for you. And I promise that the next two weeks are going to fly by *and* that you are going to have an amazing time." His kiss is long and tender.

After loading my car and giving Brian a quick kiss, I am off on the *adventure of a lifetime* according to my fiancé. And I can't help but wonder if I'm kissing my career goodbye with a travel feature.

Chapter 16

I meet Tom in the parking lot of Monroe Zoo in Michigan City, Indiana—*not*, in fact, a city in Michigan at all, but a medium-sized metropolitan city just far enough from Chicago to make travel to the city a pain unless one takes the South Shore Train Line. When my college roommate came to visit me in Chicago, her parents would drop her off at the Carroll Avenue Station in Michigan City, and she'd be at her Chicago stop with me in approximately an hour and a half without having to fight the horrendous I-80/94 traffic I'd had to battle today, even though we are way off vacation peak season in early November.

"Hi, Meg," he says a little too cheerfully. "How was your drive?"

"Aside from avoiding not one, but *two*, near misses, I'd say it was a success. How about you?"

"Great. Anita sent cookies, so they kept me happy all the way here." He laughs and pats his belly, roundish from his wife's good cooking and his inability to say no at the dinner table or to car snacks.

"Perfect. Will Anita be joining us soon? I'm so glad the producers agreed to let her tag along."

"She's going to join us when we get up to Sleeping Bear Dunes and finish the trip with us. She has some things to do in the city over the next few days, but we shall see her soon. Until then, it's just you and me, kid." He smiles warmly, a calming presence, like the older brother I never had.

I check my Apple Watch. After texting Brian quickly, we walk to the entrance of the zoo. The zoo director, Angel Cribbett, is waiting for us. She directs us to the new monkey house first. I have to resist the urge to plug my nose when we walk inside. The monkeys seem happy to see us, however much they stink. I tape a segment for Chicago Midday.

After I am done and Tom has shut off the camera, Angel brings us to the next location for our shoot. "I have a great idea!" she says with a giant smile on her face. "We are thrilled that you have made this trip to highlight our little zoo for all of Chicagoland. It is quite an honor," she beams. "We just had a baby sloth born. Would you like to see it?"

"Who can say *no* to a baby sloth?" Tom says enthusiastically.

"I agree," I say, relaxing for the first time today. I have to admit this assignment beats covering a drunk driving accident or pretend-gushing over a new way to cook broccoli.

The sloth, named CeCe Cecelia S. Sloth, a contest winner name submitted by a local third grader, is sleeping in its mother's arms when Tom turns on the camera.

"We are here at Monroe Zoo in Michigan City, Indiana, an hour's drive from downtown Chicago visiting the newest resident of the zoo—an adorable baby sloth named CeCe Celc…" At that moment, Mama Sloth swings closer from her perch in a tree, pressing her baby up against the glass partition separating us. "Well, whoa! This is…this is so cool," is all I can manage to get out before she swings back to her tree limb. "Well, I think Mama wanted baby CeCe to make her debut front and center for you all to see. The zoo will be open this fall until December 10th. Check it out for yourself. And when you are done at the zoo, be sure to visit the beautiful shores of Lake Michigan along the Indiana coastline with a viewing of one of many lighthouses we are sure to see on this trip around the lake."

"That was great, Meg," says Tom.

"I have never seen anything like that before," says Angel as she stands with her hands on her hips looking between Mama and baby sloth and me and back again. "It's like she knew she was making a commercial."

"Not quite a commercial," I say.

"Okay, if you don't like that term, then how about this? You are making a visual love letter to the communities and people along Lake Michigan so everyone in your viewing area sees how great we are and what we have to offer, even when it's not in the heat of the summer."

All I can do is nod my head and shake her hand while Tom says goodbye because I am so touched by this woman's assessment of what I am doing. And I realize what a crappy, poor-me attitude I've had all along.

Tom drives back to Chicago for the night, as his home is less than an hour away, but I drive on to my rental in Bridgman, Michigan. It's the first time I've exited I-94 at this location, exit 16. I fuel up at Casey's General Store—a mark of a small town like the Pizza Hut, Subway, and Dollar General I pass as I follow my GPS to my home for the next two nights. The rental is on the edge of downtown, an upper floor apartment in an old home. It's small but cute with a Keurig machine in the kitchen for my morning coffee before I meet Tom at Warren Dunes.

After unpacking, I call Brian. He doesn't answer but texts that he is still with Rick.

All is well. I text back.

It's only 5:30—too early to start binging Netflix on my iPad. I flip through the guidebook provided by the homeowner. I find a restaurant downtown called Lake Street Eats and More that has a nice menu. I check the reviews on Trip Advisor to be sure. I order a grilled chicken sandwich and fries to go because multiple people in the reviews claimed the french fries were *to die for.* I assume the *and More* in the restaurant's name means alcohol, but I don't want to drink alone. I pick up my order from a friendly woman at the bar and ask directions to the local beach. Another feature of a small town, she says, "Go straight through the only streetlight on this road, and you'll run right into the lake. Can't miss it."

She's right. I can't miss the stoplight, and I certainly can't miss the lake. It's gorgeous. I arrive right after sunset when the sky is still bright enough to make out the lake and beach house sitting aside the lake. The sign coming into the beach had said *Weko Beach.* I have the place to myself as I eat my grilled chicken and french fries from my car. And the reviews were right. The fries are *to die for.*

Chapter 17

It's windy and drizzling when I wake up Sunday morning for our segment at Warren Dunes, one of Michigan's most beautiful state parks between Bridgman and Sawyer, Michigan. I know I will be trudging through the sand, so I wear tennis shoes with my blue jeans and an orange pullover sweater. We are getting several segments in the can, as they say in the industry, so Chicago Midday will have spots ready to go throughout the week. We won't move out of the area until Monday night after our taping in St. Joseph.

Tom is putting a plastic tarp over the camera for our taping. The wind has picked up the closer I get to the lake. A large, almost 260-foot dune is located across the parking lot from the beach at Lake Michigan. I look to the top where small trees cling for life with a most hearty root system to still be alive in the sand. The few people who have ventured out today look like tiny dots at the top of the dune.

"Hey, Meg!" Tom waves. "You are sure lucky you didn't have to travel in this weather. I was simultaneously blown off the road and downpoured on when I crossed the state line."

"Whatever part of management thought it was a good idea to highlight this trip in the *fall* in the Midwest must really hate us."

"Naw, no hate, just bad planning. Grab an umbrella and start climbing before the rain comes back."

"Climbing? You can't be serious."

"You have to get the shot from the top, Meg. There's no point in doing a story about the great sand dunes in Michigan if you just look at them from the bottom. You have to stand on the top. Plant your flag so to speak. And I'll be right behind you—with a camera—so, go slowly."

"Ugh!" I pull off my tennis shoes because I'm discovering that it is easier to climb in the sand without shoes on, as it's not burn-your-feet kind of weather.

After ten hard minutes, I am at the top. My heart is racing but in a good workout kind of way, not an *I'm going to die* kind of way. Tom takes a few minutes more to reach me. He leans on one of the skinny trees at the top and takes several slow, deep breaths. "Are you okay?"

"Yeah…I'm…Give me another minute." While resting against the tree, he takes a bottle of water out of his pocket and takes a drink. "Okay, I'm good. Stand over there," he says, pointing to a part of the dune highlighted by the beach and lake in the background. "The waves are rocking out there. It will make a great shot."

"Hi, I'm Meg Popkin at Warren Dunes State Park in Sawyer, Michigan…"

By the time we reach the parking lot we are both wet and cold. "Want to grab a bowl of soup somewhere?" I ask.

"I'm sorry, Meg, but I told Anita I'd come back home today."

"You're driving back *again*?"

"I know. Her brother and family are in town today. It's the last time I'll drive back. Are you going to be okay by yourself?"

"Of course, Tom. No worries. I think I'll drive up to St. Joseph and scoop things out for tomorrow's taping, since it's so close. I think the rain is supposed to let up in a bit. Have fun with Anita's family."

"If you call living in hell for six hours fun." He winks at me.

"Tom! I've never heard you talk like that."

"You've never met my sister-in-law. I'll see you tomorrow at 11:00 a.m., Illinois time, for the live taping."

"Ah, yes. Good old time conversions when you cross between Central time to Eastern time. I am sure Trenton can't wait to talk to me live on camera from the co-host seat tomorrow. Do you know who is hosting with him this week?"

Tom's face drains of color. "No one told you?"

"Told me the co-host this week? Nope. I haven't heard a word. Who is it?"

"It's really not a big deal, Meg."

"Tom…"

"Can't you wait until tomorrow?"

"Tom…"

"Fine. It's Jessalyn."

"Jessalyn Bowers?" The former anchor at WDOU who used to flirt incessantly with Brian had moved on to co-host the news at WDOU's competitor station.

"It's temporary. Don't worry."

"She's perfect," I whisper. "She's an ass kisser, and that's what Trenton wants."

"Well, it's not what the show needs. Don't worry," he repeats. "Go find some soup and enjoy the quiet time. We have a lot of driving to do later this week."

Tom pats me on the forearm, puts his camera into the van, and drives away. I've suddenly lost my appetite.

I drive through a fast-food restaurant in Stevensville on my way to St. Joseph. The sun is coming out, but there is still a deep chill in the air from the wind. Fast-food soup doesn't sound appetizing, but I don't want french fries two days in a row. My willpower is much stronger than I give myself credit for sometimes.

We are taping at the Silver Beach Carousel in the morning. Tom will likely have me sitting on a carousel horse for the segment. I imagine Trenton laughing hysterically as I raise my voice to be heard over the campy merry-go-round music. I find a parking spot easily in downtown St. Joseph. This time of year, parking is not a problem. In the summer, the local police mark the tires of the cars with chalk to ensure they move within their two hours of allotted time, or they give out tickets, at least they used to. I remember my college roommate telling me stories of tourists arguing with her mom who'd been one of the local police with the unlucky assignment of passing out parking tickets to disgruntled visitors. I haven't seen Andi since our five-year reunion. It's not like we tried to avoid each other over the last eight years. We don't even follow each other on social media. Our lives just took different trajectories which happens sometimes. The last I knew she'd married a dermatologist and moved to Grand Rapids. I wonder if her parents still live in town.

I hadn't been completely honest with Tom. I wasn't really interested in scouting our shooting locations. I wanted to visit the library to do some research. The first thing I'd researched was if the library was even open on a Sunday. It is open, but only for three hours—an hour and a half left.

The library is in a building that boasts a plaque on the front that says 1921. Its beautiful lobby is highlighted by dark wood pillars and stained-glass windows. The lighting is muted but comfortable. A stern man at the counter points to a set of stairs that leads to the basement when I ask for the archives, annoyed that I'd disturbed his solitude. The marble stairs and curved handrails rival the architecture of the Harold Washington Library in the city.

The room is empty and dark. I flip the switch on to find two rows of file cabinets that line the wall labeled by years starting in 1925 and ending in 1995 when the digital shift was likely made. Cabinets of vintage books sit across from the file cabinets. Computers sit in the middle of the room. I pull out the manila folder I'd brought with me. The folder holds a picture of my dad when he was a toddler and his birth certificate, the surprise I discovered when cleaning out Dad's things in Blue Lake. According to the certificate, he'd been born in St. Joseph to Sarah Jackson and Gordan Lamont in December of 1960. I have no other information to go on, but I've been trained in my job that if you look hard enough you can find most anything, eventually. It's a mystery as to why Dad was adopted and why he'd never told anyone.

I start my work at the computer with an internet search for Sarah Jackson and Gordan Lamont. I'd restrained myself from exhausting the internet with searches the moment I held that birth certificate. It didn't feel right to be digging into Dad's beginning without dealing with his ending. Grief is a funny thing, and some days are harder than others. There are no distractions now—literally. I don't think anyone is even in the building right now except for the surly desk clerk. *Sarah Jackson* is a common name. It's a *very* common name in St. Joseph, Michigan. There are over 2500 searches that show up that bare a connection between a Sarah Jackson and St. Joseph. I look through obituaries, but nothing jumps out to me.

Lots of people named Sarah Jackson lived and died—nothing uncommon about that.

I switch to searches for Gordan Lamont. The Lamont name populates a lot of searches in St. Joseph, too. The founder of Lamont Industries, a large tool manufacturing company based in St. Joseph, has the last name of Lamont for obvious reasons. Was Gordan part of *this* Lamont family? I pull up images and try to decipher if any of my dad's features matched those of the Lamonts from St. Joseph. The biography of Royce Lamont says he started the company from his garage where he welded scrap metal into tools that he'd sell to his friends—rather entrepreneurial, actually. The company is now worth 1.2 billion dollars. I find a list of Lamonts that still live in the area with ties to Lamont Industries and take notes.

A search through files from the early 1900s provides more information about the company and its founder, but nowhere do I find the name *Paul* or a connection to a Sarah Jackson.

Frustrated, I decide to have a conversation with Mr. Gloomy Pants upstairs. "Excuse me?" I ask.

The man looks up from the book he'd been reading, a western. "Yes?"

"I'm doing some research for a project, ah, about the Lamont family from St. Joseph."

"Yes?"

I can see I need to lead this conversation. "Are there any books or possibly old newspaper articles where I can further my research? Perhaps I've not found the correct file in the archives room?"

"You could use the Lamont Room. Everything about that family is kept there."

I raise my eyebrows in surprise. "The Lamonts have a *whole room*?"

"Miss, are you not from here?" Now he raises *his* eyebrows.

"I am not."

"The Lamonts own this town. They always have. Personally, I'm not on the hater side. That side reeks of jealousy, in my opinion. Without the Lamonts we would not have many of the programs and amenities that we have now. Lamont money built this town. Heck, Lamont money built this library."

"Oh, well, that's quite something, isn't it? Can you point me in the direction of the Lamont Room?"

"Sure. Follow the hall past the nonfiction section, and you will find a room in the back right corner. It's labeled. I made the labels myself," he says proudly. "I bought a metal engraving tool. Pretty cool, huh?" he asks, pulling out the handheld tool to which he is referring.

"Yes, you are quite skilled." Why did I think this was going to be easy? All of sudden, Mr. Sour Face is chatty. "Well, thank you for your help. I'll leave you to your book." I point to his novel, *The Ranch Hand Brides.*

He blushes. "My novel? Nah, I was just, uh, covering the book."

I smile as if I believe him, which I don't, and search out the Lamont Room.

Large leather chairs and ornate lamps adorn the heavily wood-paneled room. It smells like cigar smoke though no smoking is allowed in the building. Do they make cigar smoke air fresheners? The idea seems absurd. Has the ghost of Royce Lamont been here recently?

I grab the first book I see titled *Lamont Industries, a Lamont Family History*. I skim through the book looking for the name Gordan Lamont. Turns out Gordan is Royce's son. He'd attended the University of Michigan, graduating in 1962, two years after Dad had been born. He'd been employed at Lamont Industries as Chief Executive Officer with no notice of retirement or death. There are lots of ribbon cutting ceremonies and philanthropic mentions in the book but no mention of a Sarah Jackson though there was a Leo Jackson who was listed as a board member. A knock on the door startles me.

"Closing time." It's my buddy from the front desk.

"Thanks. I'll be right out."

"What are ya doing, if you don't mind me asking?"

I contemplate sharing my true intentions, but what harm could come from my sharing? I'll never see this man again. I pull out my father's birth certificate and hand it to him. "I found this birth certificate for my father when I was cleaning out his belongings after he died. I never knew he'd been adopted, and I was trying to get some information."

He scans the paper before speaking. "Whoa. Scandalous!" He takes the paper and sits down in the tallest leather-backed chair, suddenly unconcerned with closing time.

"What do you mean?"

"Well, it looks like Gordan Lamont had an illegitimate child."

"That may be true. That happened—*happens.* But why would it be scandalous?"

"Because Johnny Lamont will be the CEO of Lamont Industries, the sole heir, and if there had been knowledge about another child, well, that's just crazy. His fortune would be cut in half. This family has been above reproach all these years." He chuckles. "Think about it. Why would Gordan Lamont have had a baby that he gave up? Was he having an affair? Ooh la la. You have uncovered something juicy, Ms….?"

"Popkin, Meg Popkin."

"I'm Stuart. And, Ms. Popkin, you might be an heir to a fortune."

Chapter 18

December 1

What is December first, Lara?

Rick's surgery

Wow, that's fast.

Because it's serious

I'll help with the boys.

Thanks

How are you?

Scared

I know. I love you.

Love you, too.

I put my phone on *do not disturb* before I go live on the air. Chicago Midday showed my Michigan City and Warren Dunes segments this morning. Now I'm going to go live on the carousel—as predicted. Apparently, years ago there was an amusement park on Silver Beach in St. Joseph, and the carousel is a nod to that time.

"Tell us, Meg," says Jessalyn through my earpiece. "How did you choose the perfect horse to perch upon today?" She giggles like a toddler who's had too much sugar. And I am reminded of the last time Jessalyn Bowers interviewed me live on the air. I'd just been attacked at the train station, and she sabotaged me with the release of the video footage of the attack. I detest this woman.

"They are all beautiful, aren't they?" I say, not betraying my disgust. "Let me tell you a little about the history of Silver Beach…" I adjust my earpiece, so I can't hear her talking until I am done presenting my story. "Later in the week, look for me in another beautiful beach town along the shores of Lake Michigan."

"Thanks, Meg. We sure do miss you on set," says Trenton.

"But not *too* much," adds Jessalyn.

"Well, we are enjoying Jessalyn, of course," he says.

I imagine Trenton tapping Jessalyn's leg, but I don't know if he does or not.

"They are nauseating, aren't they?" asks Tom.

"I don't understand what management is thinking. How could this be the direction they want to take the show?"

"Hey, at least you got to ride a merry-go-round today!"

Tom pats me on the head like I'm a little girl. He always knows how to make me smile. "Yes, I did. And it was a fine horse, too," I laugh. "I'll follow you to the winery, okay?"

"Sounds good. It should be about a two-hour drive to Ludington."

"I've got my podcasts ready to go—the history of Watergate."

"Sounds riveting."

"Call if you need me to pull off at a gas station for a potty break."

"Thanks, big brother."

When I get to my car, parked on the bluff overlooking the beach and the building with the carousel, there is a note on the windshield, likely an ad for a local fundraiser or restaurant coupons. I pull the note out from underneath my windshield wipers, but the handwriting stops me from crumpling it into a ball and throwing it on my front seat. I read the note.

You deserve nothing.

I look around to see if someone is watching me, if this is some kind of weird joke, but the street is sparse due to the nip in the air. Tom is backing out the van, so I get into my car and prepare for our next stop: Ludington, Michigan.

We visit three wineries in Ludington to tape segments for tomorrow's show. I get a lesson at Four Corners Vineyard on making wine. After watching a video demonstration that the vintner showed Tom and me, we taste test different samples of wine, but only a little as we have a long drive ahead of us. Cranberry wine is my favorite.

From Ludington we drive to Glen Arbor, Michigan, another two-hour drive. Management is putting us up at an old resort right on Lake Michigan. Tom and I have adjoining rooms. I tell Tom to let me know when Anita arrives so we can go to dinner together. When I'm in my room, I change into yoga pants and an oversized t-shirt Brian had snuck in my bag. It's cheesy, but the t-shirt smells like him, and I need to feel him around me right now. That note really spooked me. I try to tell myself that maybe it was left on the wrong car or was some silly teenage prank, but after my snooping at the library and learning more about Gordan Lamont and my possible connection to the wealthy family, I wonder if someone is trying to give me a message to leave the topic alone. If only I could.

"You have got to be kidding me," Anita says as she stands at the base of Sleeping Bear Dunes outside of Glen Arbor the next morning.

"*Thank you!* Finally, there is a sane voice on this trip." I look at Tom. He is holding the camera at his side and accessing the dune that is at least 200 feet taller than the dune at Warren Dunes he'd made me climb on Sunday. "Tom, your wife talks sense."

"Yeah, she does, but you know the story will be better received if you give your report from the *top* of a Sleeping Bear Dune."

"Do *you* think you can make it to the top?"

He scans the dune as if trying to find the strength to say *yes*. "Nah, I'm not cut out to climb this beast."

"Thank the gods of common sense!"

"Good call, honey." Anita kisses her husband on the cheek.

"But I've checked the map. There are more conquerable dune trails a bit further into the park. Let's go, team!"

"Ugh!"

After work, Anita and I spend the afternoon shopping in Glen Arbor, buying cherry salsa, cherry pretzels, and cherry candies at the Cherry Republic store in town. The smell alone is glorious.

"Want to spit?" she asks after we've paid for our treats.

"Spit?"

"Yeah, they have a cherry spitting pit out back. Come on. I challenge you."

"Are you serious?"

"As serious as humidity on a hot July day!"

If Tom is like an older brother, Anita is like a crazy cousin who always dares you to do things you regret later but have a lot of fun while doing them until you have to process what you've actually done. A starting line lies perpendicular to two low wooden fences that outline the spit pit. Distance signs mark the spitter's goals. Assorted cherry pits litter the alleyway, most only a few feet in front of the starting line. "I can't believe I am going to say this, but I think Tom should record us."

"Us?" Anita asks. "No way. I don't do television."

"This was your idea. And I'm not doing it alone. Char will love it." I pull out my phone to text Tom to come with the camera before she can stop me. And for the next hour we eat cherries and spit seeds. Neither of us gets our seeds further than a few feet. I'm laughing with my friends as we split up to get into our vehicles to drive to our next stop—Traverse City.

It's a quiet drive to Traverse City, the final leaves of fall clinging to the trees. There is something to be said about taking time to appreciate what is around you. We check into our hotel that overlooks Grand Traverse Bay. Few boats illuminate the night sky on the water this time of year. I fall asleep quickly.

I stare at the new note that sits on my windshield after we have finished taping a segment from aboard a pirate ship experience in Traverse City. Great Traverse Bay had been beautiful and calm. And even in November, the temperature had been comfortable. Tom and I had donned pirate hats while Anita drank pina coladas and laughed at us from across the deck. I've been enjoying myself and the slower pace of life more than I'd thought possible. Most of the people we've met have been so friendly and welcoming, sharing their stories with us. Plus, Brian is joining us soon for the Mackinac Island leg of our trip. That's why none of this makes sense, and now I'm rattled. The first note could have been brushed off as a mistake. But this isn't a mistake.

Face your sins.

Two notes, two times in a week. Someone is following me. And I have no idea why. I stuff this note in my purse along with the first one.

A stop in Petoskey rounds out the week. We tape a live segment on a beach at Petoskey State Park. I wear overall fishing waders as Tom tapes me looking for Petoskey stones, a unique rock found in the waters of Lake Michigan, especially near the city that shares its name. The rocks are a type of fossilized coral that form an identifiable hexagon pattern that fills the discoverer with a sense of pride.

"Any luck out there?" asks Trenton as Tom zooms in on me standing in the forty-seven-degree water and bending over to look for Petoskey stones.

"Not yet, Trenton. But I won't be deterred."

"Keep up the rock hunting, Meg. You look adorable in those pant thingies you are wearing. I think I need a pair."

I ignore Jessalyn while I pan through the rocks in my hand. No luck. No Petoskey stones and my time is up. What an embarrassing waste of time. "Well, that's how it goes sometimes," I say into the camera. "Rock hunting is a bit like fishing. You have to develop patience, and sooner or later you find the big one." I smile much too large for what I am feeling inside. "But Petoskey is a beautiful town worth a visit all year round. And, you might have better luck than me with finding a treasured rock. Thanks so much, Trenton and Jessalyn. I'll see you soon!"

"Not too soon!" says Jessalyn. "Keep looking!"

Tom shuts off the camera. I close my eyes and stomp out of Lake Michigan. What a terrible live segment.

"Try not to let them get in your head, Meg," says Tom.

If only he knew all the worries that were swirling around my mind and that during that one ridiculous segment in Lake Michigan on live television in November, I'd finally felt safe. No one can hurt me on live TV, right?

Chapter 19

It's been a long week full of some really cool experiences—more than I'd thought would be possible, to be honest. We'd spent the night in Petoskey. After Anita and Tom went back to their hotel room after our shoot, I milled around in my waders a bit longer in the lake. A couple of women were hunting nearby, so I'd felt safe enough. They even pointed out an area in the water where they'd had luck finding Petoskey stones. And wouldn't you know it? I found a real beauty that I can't wait to have polished up.

I haven't shared the notes with anyone. I am looking forward to seeing Brian today. We are meeting in Mackinaw City and taking the ferry to Mackinac Island. How odd that two towns separated only by Lake Huron, the only other Great Lake on this trek than Lake Michigan, have the exact same word in their names with different spellings though the same pronunciation. *Mackinac* is pronounced the same as *Mackinaw*.

I am enjoying my second cup of coffee on this early Saturday morning on the patio of my hotel when I see Brian's car pull into the lot. I jump up from my seat and start waving like a teenager waiting to be reunited with her high school boyfriend as he walks off the basketball court.

Brian is carrying the same duffle bag he uses to stay for a stint at my apartment in Brookfield and that he's taken on our trips to Blue Lake. We really need to register for luggage before our honeymoon—that is, if we can ever focus long enough to plan the wedding.

"Hi!" I drop the pretense of being mature and run to meet him as he approaches the hotel. I throw my arms around his neck and feel my strength renewed.

"That's the kind of reception I was hoping for!" He plants a large kiss on my lips. "But I need some coffee before I can even think of giving you a proper greeting. Do you know how long it takes to get to northern Michigan from downtown Chicago?"

"Did you even go to bed after work?"

"I took a power nap and got on the road at 3:00 a.m."

"You must really love me," I say, grinning.

"That or I've gone mad."

Being with Brian is so easy. I can't wait until we are together every day as no matter the stresses of life, he sets the world right again before my head hits the pillow, even when he leaves toothpaste in the sink and *forgets* to load the dishwasher. "Come on. There's a coffee shop inside. I'll take your bag to the room while you fuel up."

Brian takes another power nap while I work on my laptop. We are supposed to meet Tom and Anita in an hour to take the ferry to Mackinac Island. I open my email from work. There are a few *We miss you, Meg* messages from fans and an email from Char complimenting our cherry pit spitting segment. She said that most of management loved the segment but to not be surprised to get a message from the team that it was *disgusting and inappropriate to show adults spitting on television.* What team? Staff from the station? Or production? I don't even care anymore. I've embraced my inner travel enthusiast. Char had told me to reach out to locals and to find other stories to cover besides the ones assigned. That is exactly what I am doing. Plus, Danni had gone on and on in a text message thanking me for the cherry treats I'd sent to the station from Cherry Republic. She was already planning a new cooking session with Michigan cherries for next summer's crop. I nearly miss the last unopened email. I don't get much spam in my work email as our server weeds it out, but it does *look* like spam.

The subject heading says *don't miss.* I don't recognize the return email address.

I nearly fall off my chair when I open the message. An ugly face appears to grow larger on the screen as the words *die, bitch* flow out of his mouth. I click out of the email and slam my laptop shut.

I jump when Brian kisses my neck from behind. I didn't know he was up. "Are you okay?"

"Yeah, yeah, everything's fine." I glance at the clock. "You'd better take a shower. We have to leave soon."

Brian arches an eyebrow and looks at me with a goofy expression that tells me he has more in mind than getting squeaky clean. "I think you could use a shower, too." He plugs his nose.

Instinctively, I lift my arms to smell my armpits. Brian bursts into laughter before I realize what he is not so subtly hinting. "Okay, but we have to make it quick. And I can't get my hair wet!"

"So many demands." He reaches down, lifts me out of my chair, and carries me into the shower. Once again, Brian dissolves all my anxieties.

Anita is wrapped up like a polar bear when we meet Tom and her at the dock to board our ferry to Mackinac Island. Tom hands her a hot chocolate, the steam lingering in the air, held there by the cool forty-degree temperatures.

"Hi, Brian." Tom pats him on the back. "Good to have some more company. These two—" He points at Anita and me and shakes his head back and forth.

"Trouble, I know," he grins. "Good to see you both again." He kisses Anita on the cheek, and despite the temperature, I think she blushes.

The ferry is a two-tiered boat that carries only people to the small island of Mackinac as no cars are allowed on the island except emergency vehicles. A world without the hustle and bustle of traffic sounds delightful and reminds me of the slow pace of life Dad enjoyed in Blue Lake.

This time of year, after the summer crowd and the leaves-changing-colors enthusiasts have gone back to their lives, the island is quiet. I've never been here, but I've watched plenty of YouTube videos to know that this island is alive with activity for several months out of the year. Chicago Midday has splurged for a stay at the Grand Hotel, the site of the filming of the beautiful 1980 time-travel film

Somewhere in Time starring Christopher Reeve and Jane Seymour. Everyone on the property must adhere to the dress code of sports coat, tie, and dress pants for men, dresses or dress pants and blouses or sweaters for women in the evening, with no belly-baring clothes or cut-off shorts during the day. Some might claim these standards to be too old-fashioned, but there is something charming about the simplicity and class of days gone by.

I pull my jacket closer to my body as Brian carries my bags. A horse-driven carriage marked with a sign saying *Grand Hotel* takes us to the hotel. Not a car in sight is a miraculous thing. Was life really simpler back in time, or did it just carry a different set of stresses?

"It's stunning," Anita says before I can get the words out myself. The hotel sits high upon a hill that overlooks the Straits of Mackinac and the Mackinac Bridge that connects the upper and lower peninsulas of Michigan, nothing but nature and beauty from every direction. The front porch boasts over 600 feet of loveliness with wonderful views. I'd like nothing more than to curl up there with a good book and a glass of wine, but work is calling.

Our first taping happens at the horse barn where I am going to interview Harold Parot, the chief horse keeper for the island. I learn that horses had been on the island since the 1700s and that automobiles had been banned around 1900, making the "Horse is King" motto created by the owner of the Grand Hotel a popular advertisement for the island. Over 600 horses live on the island during busy season while most return to mainland farms during the winter. They carry guests around the island in horse-drawn carriages and wagons for those guests that don't want to take bicycles or walk.

"This is Big Gary," I say, petting the large animal that is nuzzling my pockets, smelling out the carrot Harold had given me to use at the end of the taping. "He has been working on Mackinac Island for seven years, delighting the guests…" Big Gary can't wait any longer. He nudges a little too hard, and I drop my microphone. "Okay, buddy." I pick up my microphone, reach into my pocket, and hand him the carrot which he gratefully destroys in seconds. "Join us as we continue our travels around the island," I say to my Chicagoland viewers.

Tom shuts off his camera.

"Tom, why don't you and Anita spend some time exploring the island?" I say after we leave the horse barn. Brian and I will do the shoot at Arch Rock. That's a long way to lug your camera equipment, and Brian can use the handheld camera to tape my segment—if you don't mind, of course."

"He doesn't mind," says Anita as she slings her arm around Tom's shoulders. "Thanks, Meg. Shall me meet for dinner tonight?" Her smile is infectious.

"Yes, of course. Let's start with cocktails on the Grand Hotel porch first, though."

"You sound so fancy," says Brian. *"Cocktails."* He laughs. "No cold beer for me tonight."

Brian grabs the small camera from Tom and puts it in his backpack. I check the map to Arch Rock, a rare geological formation of limestone that overlooks Lake Huron from up high. It's one of the most visited sites on the island, so a taping there is necessary. We check out bikes from the concierge at the Grand Hotel. Brian keeps his backpack on, but I put my backpack in the wire basket that sits in front of the handlebars of my bicycle. It's a two-mile ride to Arch Rock. This time of year, the island is eerily quiet. I'm reminded that this trip to *highlight* the trip around Lake Michigan in the offseason was just a ruse to get me out of the studio because soon this island will be nearly vacant because Northern Michigan gets snow early and often, and the ferries can't travel then. I redirect my efforts to focus on the here and now with the love of my life, but the fact that I'm likely being replaced in my job lurks just below the surface.

I am freezing by the time I get to Arch Rock. We park our bikes at the base of the stairs and climb to the top—all 207 steps. The view is stunning. Lake Huron shines on this crisp, sunny fall day like tiny diamonds floating on the water. For a moment it reminds me of Blue Lake, only much larger.

"Do you know what you are going to say?" Brian asks, as he pulls up the hood on his sweatshirt.

"Do I know what I am going to say? Dude, you are dealing with a professional here."

"My apologies, dear lady." Brian bows at my feet, and I giggle like a little kid.

He takes out his camera, looks behind him to make sure he doesn't step off the cliff, and records my piece about the unique nature found on Mackinac Island.

"Brian, look!" I say after taping my segment. I hold out my hand to grab at snowflakes that have begun falling, the diamonds on the lake becoming diamonds in the sky.

"Got one! Got another one!" Brian bounces around with his tongue hanging out like a giraffe at the feeding station of a zoo and catches snowflakes on the tip of his tongue.

I grab his hand and pull him close to me, the warmth of our bodies coming together. "Have I told you how much I love you?"

"Truth be told, I think you might have left that out—*today*."

"Well, I do, and I vow to make sure I tell you that every day for the rest of our lives."

"Does that mean I can nail you down to talking about wedding plans?" He tips up my chin so that I am looking in his eyes.

"I'm sorry. I promise that as soon as this advent—*misadventure*—whatever it is, is over, I'll focus on planning the wedding." I kiss him on the lips.

"Not good enough, Meg. You have time without me annoying you in the evenings during the week. At least do some Google searches and see if anything in the wedding planning realm excites you, okay? I want to make this permanent sooner than later. I'm ready to wake up to you every day as my wife."

He kisses me tenderly, and I melt. I snuggle into his hoodie as the snowflakes fall gently around us. What a perfect day.

Chapter 20

When we get back to the hotel to freshen up for cocktails and dinner, the message light on our room phone is blinking, the old-fashioned, plug-in-the-wall type of phone that you don't see much anymore unless you are staying somewhere *vintage*.

"What's that for?" Brian asks as he removes his shirt to take a shower.

"Probably Char couldn't reach me on my cellphone—bad reception, I imagine."

"Want to join me in there?" Brian asks, pointing to the bathroom.

"I'll pass, for now. I better get this message."

"Your loss," he says with a sly smile as he takes off his jeans.

I sit on the edge of the bed. "Brian, have you been watching Chicago Midday?"

"I've seen a bit of it, not an entire show. Just keeping tabs for my girl, you know?"

I nod my head. "And…how is Jessa doing—with Trenton?" I dread the answer but need to know.

Brian sits down next to me in his underwear. He takes my hand in his. "Meg, watching Jessa and Trenton together is like watching a swarm of flies devour horse shit. It's repulsive and drips of fakeness. They may have chemistry, but it is *not* enjoyable to watch. She actually held onto his back as he did squats in an exercise segment. It was nauseating."

"Okay, that's, well, I guess that's good. But…what…what if that's what the audience wants?"

"The audience wants authenticity and empathy and fair, factual, entertaining delivery. All Jessa and Trenton have together is sex appeal. Sex sells and all, but it doesn't make for a news and entertainment show in the middle of the day."

"Okay. Thanks." I look up and see the sweetest concern in Brian's eyes. "Maybe we could muss up the bed a bit before your shower?"

"I think that is a fabulous idea."

Brian scoops me off the end of the bed. I wrap my legs around his strong abdomen. He holds me there while we kiss before pulling back the comforter and gently laying me on the bed. He pulls off my sweater and kisses me gently starting at the top of my forehead down to my breasts where he removes my bra. His intentions increase in intensity as I wriggle out of my underwear. And somewhere over the next five minutes I lose myself as we become one.

Brian rolls over to my side of the bed after he wakes up from his nap. "I think we're going to be late for cocktails," he grins. "I still have to take that shower."

I look up from my phone where I'd been scrolling for the last fifteen minutes. "All good. I texted Tom and Anita that we'd meet them at 6:00 instead of 5:15. But you'd better get in that shower, so I can take one, too."

"Okay. He kisses me on the tip of my nose, and I watch him walk naked into the bathroom.

I push the button with the blinking light on the phone, expecting to hear Char's chastisement that I haven't checked in today. I've had too much fun pretending I was on vacation to bother with communicating with Chicago Midday. But it's not Char on the phone.

I know where you are. I know what you're doing. Time to give up.

I drop the phone receiver. It hits the bedside table with a loud thud. I get up to pull the room's drapes. Someone is here. Or someone *was* here. Or someone knows I am here. What is going on? I can't ignore the messages anymore.

We huddle around the outdoor heaters on the front porch of the Grand Hotel as we enjoy cocktails and appetizers—stuffed crab, sausage rolls, and baked feta bites. Anita and I are wearing our winter jackets over our Grand Hotel finest while Tom and Brian are wearing suits. What should be an amazing cap off to a wonderful day is about to be squelched, but I need to tell them what is happening.

After we order dinner at the Island Inn, a block away from the hotel, I take a long drink of wine before starting my difficult conversation. "I have something to tell you." I take another drink.

Three sets of eyes turn their attention to me. "What's up, babe?" asks Brian.

"Are you two eloping on the island?" Anita asks, her eyes twinkling with merriment.

I take a deep breath. "I wish it were something beautiful like that. But it is not. So…something weird has been happening on the trip."

"What's wrong, Meg? I haven't noticed anything unusual."

"That's good, Tom. I mean, I'm glad you haven't seen any problems. But…"

Brian lays his hand on top of mine. "What is it?"

I pull the two notes out of my purse and hand them to Brian.

"*You deserve nothing. Face your sins.*" He reads aloud the two notes that had been placed upon my windshield.

"What do these mean?"

"I wish I knew. The first note showed up on my car in St. Joseph the day I did some exploring around the city after Tom went home. I blew it off, assuming it was a stupid teenage prank or perhaps meant for someone else. But then the second note appeared on my car in Traverse City."

"What the hell?" Brian pounds the table. "Meg, this is serious. Why didn't you…?"

"Wait. There's more," I whisper.

"Meg, what do you mean?" Tom shows the same concern as Brian but restrains his emotions.

"I also got an email sent to my work account."

"What did it say?" asks Brian.

I describe the face that grew on the screen with the words *die, bitch.* Before anyone can react, I continue talking. "And today, on our hotel room phone, there was a message."

"I thought you said it was Char."

"I said I *thought* it was Char," I pause. "But it wasn't." I hold up my phone and push the play button on the video feature where I'd recorded the hotel's phone message.

I know where you are. I know what you're doing. Time to give up.

After the message has played, I look at the faces of my friends. Anita and Tom look sullen and confused with wrinkled foreheads. Brian looks angry. His face is red, and his fists are clenched. "We are going to the police right now." He pushes his chair away from the table.

"Brian, sit down." I grab hold of his arm and tug on it. "We are on an *island.* There is low crime here. Wait until we are back on the mainland. And what can we do? The messages have appeared in multiple jurisdictions."

"Then we contact the state police. Meg, someone is threatening you. This is serious. And why the hell didn't you tell me?"

It's the first time Brian has yelled at me since he was out of his mind with worry about his sister and niece who were caught in the Chicagoland Science Museum during a mass shooting earlier in the year, but I know it only comes from a deep place of love. "I'm sorry. I didn't want to bother anyone. I've got a tight schedule to adhere to. I don't have time to *play victim* as Trenton likes to say about me."

"To hell with Trenton. You are not *playing victim*."

"Brian is right, Meg. *Being a victim* and *playing victim* are two very different things."

"You poor thing," Anita says, squeezing my hand. "Tom, have you noticed anything odd? Anyone following you guys?"

Tom shakes his head back and forth. "No, no. I haven't noticed a thing. Can you read the messages again, back-to-back?"

You deserve nothing.

Face your sins.

Die, bitch.

I know where you are. I know what you're doing. Time to give up.

"What do you think it means?" Tom asks, turning to Brian.

"I have no idea. Meg?"

I shake my head. "I can't think of anything, except…"

"Yes?" Brians says.

"I gave a victim impact statement last year that the judge used in deciding his sentences for those kids that attacked me on the train platform. But how would they know where I was on this trip? Or what my car looks like?"

"Well, your schedule can't be too hard to figure out," says Anita. "The show's really pushing this feature. They are always telling the viewers what towns are coming up during the week."

"What about my car?"

"Someone's watching you," Brian says. "Someone has been stalking you, watching your every move. How else would someone know exactly where you are all the time?"

"We don't know that it's *all the time*," I say, trying to sound more positive.

"Did you say the notes started in Michigan City?"

"No, that's the weird thing. Nothing happened in Michigan City or at Warren Dunes. It started in St. Joseph."

"What were you doing right before you found the note in St. Joseph?" asks Tom.

The waitress arrives at our table with a giant smile on her face. "Here you go, folks," she says as she deposits our dinner plates before us, whitefish all around with steaming garlic mashed potatoes and green beans.

I'm the only one that smiles back. "Thank you." I look at my friends. "Come on, guys. Dig in!" I try to lighten the mood. It doesn't work. No one touches their dinner.

"Answer the question, Meg," says Brian.

"What question?" All I want to do is eat and forget about the messages. This isn't how this night was supposed to go.

"What were you doing right before you found the note in St. Joseph?" Tom repeats.

I sigh. "When Brian and I were cleaning Dad's things out of his condo in Blue Lake, we found a birth certificate for my dad, only it wasn't the birth certificate I expected. There was a different set of parents listed, meaning Dad might have been adopted though Lara and I never knew. The birthplace was listed as St. Joseph, Michigan, so I went to the library to do some research, see if I could find any information about the people listed on the document."

"Did you find anything?" Brian takes a second to take a drink of his beer.

"Everyone, please eat your dinner. We can talk about this later."

"Meg!" Anita raises her voice for the first time. "Girl, tell us what you found out. The whitefish can wait."

"I didn't find any information on my dad's biological mother, Sarah Jackson, but I found a lot of information about Gordan Lamont, his biological father. Gordan's father Royce founded Lamont Industries."

"*Lamont Industries?* The tool manufacturer?" asks Brian.

"Yes, though I can't say *I've* heard of the company." I laugh, but no one else does.

"So, are you saying that Paul's biological father was the son of the founder of Lamont Industries?" Brian asks.

"It seems that way."

"Is he still alive?" asks Anita.

"He is, actually. He's in his 80s."

"Does he have any children?" Anita asks.

"He does. He has one son."

"Wrong," says Tom.

"Because Paul was also his son," Brian finishes Tom's thought. "Which makes *you*, as an heir of Paul, entitled to a possible fortune when Gordan Lamont dies."

"That's ridiculous. I don't want a fortune."

"Your grandfather is a billionaire, Meg. You might have rights whether you want them or not," says Tom.

"Well, I don't think I have any rights. Even if you are correct about the money, and I am not saying you are because Dad was adopted and raised by *another family*, I don't want it. And how in the world does this relate to the notes I've been getting?"

"Because someone might *think* you want money. Did anyone know what you were doing at the library?" asks Brian.

"Of course not. Well…I talked to the librarian. He was a dowdy, moody guy although he did light up when I told him what I was doing. But why would he leave me notes? That's just silly." I pick up my fork and take a bite of mashed potatoes. They are flavorful. And cold. "No more talking. Eat." I end the conversation.

Chapter 21

Brian had spent the night switching between being super crabby with me because I didn't tell him sooner about the messages I'd received to smothering me with worried attention. I didn't like either disposition. I don't want to be treated differently. I don't want to be a *victim* again. No amount of protestations can convince me that Trenton isn't correct—that I get off on being the victim with the recognition and pity I get from the audiences who watch me. The last thing I want is for him or the studio to get wind of this mess. But I am not going to persuade Brian to skip a visit to the state police station in St. Ignace.

St. Ignace is across the mighty Mackinac Bridge. I insist on recording my visit across the bridge starting on the Mackinaw City side spanning five miles over the Straits of Mackinac. The bridge was constructed in 1957 connecting the Upper Peninsula and Lower Peninsula of Michigan. Truth be told, I am glad Brian is going to drive across the bridge today. It will give me more courage to do it myself when Tom and I set out on the next part of our trip tomorrow. I'm grateful to Char for giving us the weekend on Mackinac Island. At least there's that.

"Don't forget to tell them everything," Brian says as we are in the middle of the bridge, passing a semi-truck on its left.

"I didn't think about semis traveling over the bridge, but it makes sense."

"Meg, stop it. Focus!"

"I am focused—on staying alive on this bridge."

"Well, I am staying focused on keeping you alive *off* the bridge, too."

I take a deep breath. "I promise that I will tell the police everything." I put my hand on Brian's knee, and he kicks his leg as if I'd hit him with a doctor's hammer in the special spot on the knee used to test for reflexes. His nerves are on high alert. "Trust me. It's going to be okay."

"How can you know that?" He turns to look at me.

"Eyes on the road! Because I just do. Everything is okay when you're around."

"I'm going back to Chicago tomorrow. I think you should come, too."

"You can't be serious!" I stare at the middle supports of the bridge, too nervous to look to the massive lake below.

"Meg, you could be in real danger. Someone is trying to give you a message."

"No one is telling me to stop taping filler pieces about small town America."

"True, but this started only after you began this trip."

"It doesn't mean there's a connection. You have to trust me. I will be careful. Tom has already promised you that he will follow me every time I get in the car. There will always be someone watching over me."

Brian's knuckles are turning white and not because he's still got a half mile to go on the Mighty Mac. "I don't like it. And…and your dad wouldn't like it, either."

"Low blow."

"I know. I'm sorry. I just…Meg, the last time someone went after you I about went out of my mind. I don't want to imagine a world without you."

"You will be stuck with me, for better or worse." I squeeze his hand.

We pull into the parking lot of the Michigan State Police Department. I give a full account of everything that's been happening to me since first finding the note in St. Joseph. State Trooper Samuelson is a no-nonsense older woman. She doesn't empathize or comment on the effects of these threats on my mental health, but she asks all the right questions and makes a thorough account of my experiences.

"Ms. Popkin, I can assure you that we take these threats seriously. There are a few possible theories. Your stalker is interested in you because of your public persona."

"But I'm not anywhere near Chicago which is my viewing market."

"True, but I assume your travel segments are being highlighted on the show, perhaps even mapped out on their website?" She straightens her glasses as she reviews her notes.

"Yes, I think my itinerary is being posted."

"In addition to the public personal stalker theory, another possibility is that there is someone close to you—someone who has a vendetta—who is trying to leave some kind of message. Can you think of someone who might have a grudge—whether justified or not—against you?"

I shake my head vehemently. "No, of course not."

"She's a very kind, easy-going person," Brian adds.

"Uh-huh. Ms. Popkin, do you mind if I ask you a few more questions—alone?" She glances confidently at Brian, defying him to argue.

"I don't understand why that would be nec…"

"It's fine," says Brian, touching my hand gently. "I'll go find some coffee for us. Take your time." He smiles at Trooper Samuelson as he walks past her and out of the room. She doesn't smile back.

"Ms. Popkin, who *personally* knows about your intimate travel itinerary?"

"As in, where I am staying, etc.? Because anyone who checks the website knows where I am headed next, as we have already established."

"That is what I mean." She taps her pen on the clipboard holding my report.

"Brian, my camera operator Tom, his wife Anita, my boss Char, and any necessary staff at Chicago Midday who have helped to organize this trip. Oh! And my sister Lara."

"And do *any* of those people hold a special threat?"

"Of course not! No way." I shake my head adamantly. "Though I understand your question, Trooper Samuelson, they are all safe people."

She doesn't say anything but makes a note on my report. "I want you to let your employers know that they need to remove your schedule from their website. No one except for those absolutely necessary need to know about what you are doing and where you are going. How much longer is your travel assignment?"

"I have another week."

"Okay. It will be interesting to see if things stop happening when you return home. You can't let your guard down, even when you are back in Chicago. Get a security camera for your front and back doors. Carry pepper spray with you. Be aware of your surroundings. Make sure…"

I tune out as she continues to list security measures. PTSD takes over as I'd been told all the same things after my train platform attack. To think that I am in another possible position of harm is unbelievable, and I hate it. When she has stopped speaking, I nod my head as if I agree with everything she's said. "Thank you."

"Please be in touch if anything else happens to you while you are in Michigan. If you have problems in Wisconsin or when you are back in Illinois, please notify me as well, and I will catch the police stations there up to date so we can coordinate our information."

"Thank you for your help."

"Be safe out there, Ms. Popkin. It's a scary world."

Don't I know it.

Chapter 22

I call Lara from the car as Tom follows me to our first and only stop in the Upper Peninsula. Char has decided that since the UP's winter starts sooner and quicker and it's already November, the reality of our viewership traversing there anytime soon is not reasonable. Duh! I could have told her that when she tried to sell me so hard about how our segments would send a rush of people to immediately walk in my footsteps. Regardless, I'm excited to visit Kitch-Iti-Kipi, Michigan's largest natural freshwater spring. The UP is gorgeous.

"How is Rick?" I ask, having already decided that I am not going to tell her about the threats.

"He's scared," she whispers as if she's trying to keep the boys from hearing her side of the conversation.

"I'm sorry, Lara."

"We've gone in for pre-surgery appointments. That man has gotten so much blood drained for tests it's a miracle he has any left."

"It will be a good Christmas. You'll see."

"Or not."

"A wise friend once told me something helpful," I say, remembering Brian's words to me during a hard time.

"You don't have enough faith yourself to know that things are going to turn out, so I'm sharing my faith with you. And you can give it back when you know that everything I've said was true."

"You always think you're right." She isn't sassy, just sad.

"I know, but will you take my faith anyway?"

"I will. Thanks. I have to go. Scooter is digging a hole in the backyard, and Nolan is throwing dirt at his brother."

After we pull into the parking lot of Kitch-Iti-Kipi, Tom does a thorough eagle-eyed assessment of our surroundings. The lot is empty except for one car which I assume belongs to Amy Horton, the ranger at Palms Book State Park who oversees Kitch-Iti-Kipi.

"Incredible. Just incredible," says Tom as we stare at the amazing emerald green water.

"I've never seen water this color. It's stunning."

Ms. Horton directs us to the wooden raft that is self-powered by turning a wheel that moves the raft across the water to the other side as it passes slowly along a cable. "What kinds of fish are those?" I ask, pointing to the middle bottom of the raft where there is an opening to view the crystal-clear water.

"Those are trout," says Ms. Horton. "Aren't they beauties?"

"They're huge."

"They love it here. The water maintains nearly a forty-five-degree temperature all year long."

When we are halfway across the spring, we tape the rest of the segment touting the beauty of the UP. I finish the interview with Ms. Horton while Tom pans to the water. The trees have dropped their leaves, but I can imagine what it must look like in the early days of fall.

"Thanks for your time, Ms. Horton."

"And thank you for recording a beautiful part of our state. Come back again when it's a bit warmer." She laughs.

"I will be back."

Following Ms. Horton's recommendation for lunch, we leave this quiet piece of paradise to drive to the restaurant. During a lunch of a beef and potato pasty, another favored treat in northern Michigan and Wisconsin, a meal in a pastry shell filled with meat and vegetables, I turn the camera on Tom to record his reactions to the tasty treat.

"Best meal I've had all year," he says through a mouthful of warm food.

We say goodbye to the beautiful state of Michigan and head to the next leg of our trip: Wisconsin. Relieved to be free of any new threats, I hope I'm leaving the odd experiences behind and chalk them up to a mentally unstable fan's reaction to something I've possibly said or done.

The rest of today is hours of driving as we are spending two nights in Door County, a wonderful peninsula on the east coast of Wisconsin along Lake Michigan. We are recording at Cave Point County Park near Sturgeon Bay tomorrow. The high temperature is supposed to be 35 degrees, part of the reason why Char has limited our Wisconsin stops. The weather is quickly changing, and not much looks good on tape or in person on a cloudy, windy, dark day.

I glance in my rearview mirror, comforted by Tom's presence in the Chicago Midday van following closely behind. Brian has called three times during this drive. I appreciate his concern, but it's also a bit smothering. I don't want to be perceived as a victim. The phone rings. It's Char.

"Hey, Char."

"Hi, Meg. Where are you right now?"

"I'm in the car. We will be in Sturgeon Bay in an hour."

"Good. Hey, I wanted to let you know a couple of things. First, I took down your specific itinerary from the website like you asked. Have you had any more problems?"

"Nope. No problems."

"Good. The second thing I wanted to tell you about before you see it on social media is that Jessalyn had an *accident* on the air today."

"What happened?" I grip the steering wheel a little tighter.

"We don't exactly know yet. She stood up after an interview with a local artist, and she collapsed."

"Oh no! Is she okay?"

"She's being assessed at the hospital. She's conscious. She hit her head on the coffee table on set when she went down."

"That's terrible. Were there any signs of problems earlier in the day?"

"Not at all. She went to the preproduction meeting with Trenton, got hair and makeup with Becca, and wardrobe with Clive. She did a cooking segment with Danni—Thanksgiving Day appetizers. Then she had the interview on the couch and down she went."

"Do you…do you need me to come back early?" I can't believe I am asking, afraid of Char's answer.

"No, Meg. I mean…we miss you. We really do. But you're doing a great job with your travel segment. Ratings are really good, and I think you are a huge part of that. But, well, the consensus is that we should keep testing personalities with Trenton. I wasn't going to tell you, but you deserve the truth."

"Do you mean that even when I get back from my trip around Lake Michigan, I still might not get my job back?"

"I…I don't know. You're not being fired, of course, but you might be…"

"Don't say reassigned. Don't you dare say reassigned, Char." I click the end button on the call. I don't care for a second that I've just hung up on my boss.

I bid Tom goodnight as soon as we are checked into our hotel in Sturgeon Bay. It has been a long day. I am exhausted, physically and emotionally. We'd gone through the drive-through at Jimmy Johns, so I plan on watching a stupid cable TV movie and eating my sub sandwich in the middle of my king-size bed to clear my thoughts. But the universe has other plans for me as I receive a text message.

Hey. This is Stuart from the library in St. Joe. I have some news you might like to hear. Call me, please. 555-269-2861

I don't recall giving Stuart my number, but perhaps I did. It was an overwhelming bit of information I was learning about the Lamont family. I should eat my sandwich and watch a rom com movie, but my curiosity wins. I take a few bites of my sandwich, close the blinds, make sure my deadbolt is locked on the door, and call Stuart.

"Hello," the voice on the other end of the line says as lackluster as the first time I'd spoken with him at the library.

"Hi. This is Meg Popkin. You sent me a message to call you."

"Oh, yes! Meg! Thanks for calling," he says, suddenly energized.

"You mentioned that you had some news for me."

"Yes, I do. But first, I must tell you how much I am enjoying your show. You are nailing your descriptions of every place you have visited. That cherry pit spitting contest was hilarious!"

"Uh, thanks. It was fun."

"Yes, I've done it myself, with my partner. Anyway, I thought you might like to know that Gordan Lamont has died."

"I'm sorry to hear that. It must be quite a loss for the community."

"Ah, yes. Mr. Lamont was very generous with his money, but now Johnny Lamont will become the sole heir, and he is—let's just say—*not* a beacon of shining light in the community. He's rude and self-important. And a very close friend of mine says he's heard that Johnny might not even be the true bio son of Gordan, that his wife may have already been pregnant with him when they met."

"Okay. Listen, Stuart, I really don't understand what any of this has to do with me."

"Well, if my source is correct, then *you,* Meg Popkin, may be the true heir to the Lamont Industries' fortune."

It's at this moment that I remember the Harley-Davidson ad found with Dad's things in Blue Lake in the same box as the one with his birth certificate. On the back had been written the name, *Johnny L.* with a phone number. Had Dad made contact with the man that would have been his half-brother?

"Again, that's interesting and all, but I have no desire to seek a fortune from the possible biological father of my dad. He was raised by a delightful family in Wisconsin. They were wonderful grandparents to my sister and me. This Johnny man, whether he's a saint or a sinner, is really of no concern. He is the only true heir."

"Well, I was afraid you might say that. So, um, well, I…"

"Yes?" My patience is growing thin, and my stomach is growling.

"I may have made a call to the local paper…about you. And you might be receiving a call from a reporter."

"You did *what?*" I yell into the phone. I pick up the remote control and slam it up and down on the bed.

"You seemed like a nice lady. I was doing my due diligence making your presence known to the community.

It's a real good reporter, too, a Mr. Van Winkle. I know, I know, the name is lame, but he's a great reporter."

"I will *not* take any calls from Mr. Van Winkle or any other fairy tale character. You had no right to bring me into this story. Hell, it's not even a story of known facts. My research is still pure speculation."

"I did some digging, too, Meg. I think your speculation about your dad being Gordan Lamont and Sarah Jackson's child was truth. Sarah Jackson was the daughter of Leo Jackson, a board member at Lamont Industries. I suspect that when Gordan knocked up Leo's daughter years ago, the trade-off for him keeping his mouth shut was to gain a lifetime position on the board, which is what he had until he died in a car accident three years ago."

I can't speak. How dare this man use *my* dad to promote *his* selfish intentions of publicly humiliating some guy and casting doubt on his rightful inheritance from a tool making company for goodness' sake! I click the end button on this call for the second time today.

Chapter 23

Cave Point County Park is overcast, wet, and cold. The wind passes through all of my many layers. There is an observation tower we were set to climb to get an aerial shot of Lake Michigan, but it's so foggy we know we won't be able to see a thing. Instead, we carefully step over giant wet rocks that jut out over the lake to make an interesting backdrop for my story. This Wisconsin side of Lake Michigan, though beautiful to be sure, is much different in its topography. These giant rocks are much more common here compared to the sandier beaches across the lake in Michigan. People have been known to do rock jumping here though cases of accidents always accompany these stories. I've been risk-averse my whole life, and I am not about to change that now.

As we approach a level spot on the rocks with as good of a backdrop as we can get in the fog, I hear a quiet curse behind me.

"Dammit!"

I look behind me to see Tom bending over holding his ankle. "Are you okay?"

"Yeah, I'll be fine, just a little slip on these rocks."

"Should we turn back?"

"No. Let's get this segment in the can. We have a live shot to do later in town at the jelly shop."

After recording our segment, I have to help Tom back across the rocks. He leans against my shoulder while I hold his camera with my outside hand. It's a slow walk back to the parking lot.

"I think you should go get that looked at," I say, pointing to Tom's ankle which is already swelling.

"I'll be fine."

But a quick look at Tom's face says he's very much *not* fine as he cries out in pain when he tries to show me that he can put weight on the ankle.

"Sure, you are." I pull out my phone and Google *walk-in clinics.* "There's a clinic in Jacksonport. Have them wrap you up and give you some pain meds. We have plenty of time to record at the jelly shop. I'll let them know we may be a little late."

Tom stares at me as he leans against the van.

"Stop it. I know what you are thinking, but I am a big girl." I wave my arms around the foggy vista of the county park. "No one is here today. We are completely alone."

"But I promised Brian that I would never take my eyes off of you when we were out and about."

I put my hand gently on Tom's arm. "I know. And you've done a great job watching over me, but I am fine. I am safe. And you'll be no help to me fending off crazy stalkers if you can't chase after them." I laugh, but Tom doesn't.

"Are you sure, Meg?"

"Tom! Go! You are wasting time. You can watch me get into my car. See." I point to my car. "Here I go," I say exaggeratedly. "I'm going to call into work and talk to Char, and then I will be on my way. Text me when you are done!"

Tom sighs as he opens the van door. He doesn't drive away until he sees me get into my car.

I punch in Char's number, hoping that the wi-fi will hold out long enough for me to get some questions answered about our next locations and an update on Jessalyn. Plus, I can't help but wonder who is sharing a co-hosting spot with Trenton now that Jessa's out.

"Hi, Meg," Char says in an inflated effort at being happy to hear my voice. I suppose she's still angry that I hung up on her before.

I know she's not the one making the decisions about the co-host position, but I still hold a grudge. "Hi, Char. How's Jessa doing?"

"Oh, well, she's out of the hospital."

"That's good. Did the doctors figure out what happened—why she collapsed?"

"Not so far. It's odd, but she's resting at home now."

"Good. I'm glad to hear she's better." I hate Jessalyn Bowers, but I don't wish ill will on very many people. "I was wondering if you could share the contact information for the Wisconsin Maritime Museum in Manitow…what the hell?"

"Meg? Are you okay?"

"I don't…" The call drops at the same time my car is being rammed from behind a second time. I fumble for my keys, wishing I had a new car with a fob and didn't need to always search through my abyss of a purse. I find my keys in the bottom of my purse, but before I can get them in the ignition, my car starts moving forward, no longer being rammed but now being pushed. A quick glance in the rearview mirror shows a large black pickup truck. The number of feet between my car in the parking lot and the depths of Lake Michigan gets smaller and smaller with the truck's steady pressure against my little car.

My mind is like a ping pong game. If I stay in my car, I might plummet into the lake. If I jump out of my car, I might… My neck snaps forward after a robust attack by the truck on my bumper. Fight or flight kicks in. What the hell is happening? I glance in the rearview mirror again, the truck inching me closer and closer to the edge of the land separating my car from the parking lot and Lake Michigan. I can't stay here. I throw my purse over my body, shove my phone inside, open the car door, and run. I run for a trail behind the parking lot I'd seen when Tom and I arrived. The name, Ascension Trail, had caught my attention. I don't dare turn back. All I hear are my own breaths that get heavier and heavier the further I run. A T in the path panics me, but I turn north because that's the direction of the road that led into the county park. Every part of my body and mind aches when I get to the road. What if the black truck is waiting there for me—knowing that I'd take this route? What if someone is coming down the trail behind me? My angels are watching out for me as I don't have long to wait before I hear something coming down the road. I duck behind the large trunk of a tree that stands near the road. I peek around the tree and see a red jeep getting closer. With one last glance behind me, I run to the side of the road and start waving my arms like a madwoman, jumping up and down. The jeep slows down enough that I can see it is an older man and woman inside. They pass by me but stop and back up a few yards down the road.

I run to the door of the man who sits in the driver's seat. He rolls down the window. "I need help. I need…" I put my hand on the jeep to steady myself.

"What's the matter, miss?" The man has a kind voice.

I shiver involuntarily. "I…truck…I…there's a truck…oh my God!" I yell, pointing at a black truck that is turning out of the park entrance ahead of us. I cower to the ground instinctively.

"Henry! Do something for her. She's terrified."

The elderly man opens the door of his jeep, gets out, opens the back door, and helps me inside."

"Here, hon. Take this blanket." The soft-spoken, old woman hands me a fleece blanket from her lap. "You are drenched. You must be freezing, honey."

"Thank you. I…that man... He…he was trying to push my car from the parking lot to…"

"Somebody was trying to push your car into *Lake Michigan*?" asks the woman.

All I can manage is a shake of my head, my energy and adrenaline waning. "Can you take me to the police station please?"

"Of course, sweetie. You rest. We will take you into Jacksonport. You rest your eyes."

Officer Davids is talking on the phone to State Trooper Samuelson, the Michigan State Trooper who took my last police report. I guess the warning messages didn't stop in Michigan after all. Wisconsin just made them a lot harder to downplay. I pull my phone out of my purse. There are twenty-five messages. Oh no. I forgot that I'd been talking to Char in the park. There are also messages from Brian and Tom.

Meg, answer.

Meg, are you okay?

Char called. She can't get ahold of you. Everything okay?

Call me immediately.

What happened? Are you okay?

I read all of the messages, all variations of the one before. I sigh. I text each of them the same message.

I am okay. I'll explain later.

Then I call Tom and ask him to meet me at the Jacksonport Police Station when he is done at the doctor's office.

"Ms. Popkin," says Officer Davids.

"Meg."

"Meg, I'm sorry this happened to you today. I am sure you are pretty shaken up."

It's refreshing to have some empathy in person. Tears fall freely from my eyes, and I wipe them away with the back of my hand. "It's been a crazy day—*week*."

"Yes, I understand that. Trooper Samuelson gave me an update. The FBI is going to be involved now that these crimes are likely related and cross state lines."

"The FBI?" Trenton is going to *love* rubbing that in my face, like I'm needing an FBI investigation to up my victim card game, or whatever he thinks I'm doing.

"I'm afraid so. This is serious. Your car has been photographed at the scene. You were one foot away from plunging into Lake Michigan. That's attempted murder."

"Murder?" My mouth feels dry, and my tongue sticks to the roof of my mouth so it comes out more like *murther*. I accept a bottle of water from Officer Davids.

"Ms. Popkin, there's someone here who'd like to see you," a young man says from the doorway to Officer Davids' office.

"Meg!"

"Tom!"

I start crying again as I fall into a welcome hug from someone who loves me like family.

I sleep all the way back to Chicago. Char has called off our trip, sending us home. I'm disappointed yet also relieved. I don't know what is going on, why I am being followed, what I have done to make someone want to hurt me, or worse yet, *kill* me.

I wake up when Tom pulls the van in front of Brian's condo, my car having been impounded for evidence. I still haven't talked to him myself. I wasn't ready for the smothering concern—not yet. I'm too tired. But Tom has talked to everyone that had heard of my *incident*: Char, Brian, and Lara. I feel terrible that my experiences have been added to her list of worries, but Char had communicated with all my contacts when she couldn't reach me after our call was cut off amidst my screams.

Brian has taken the rest of the day off to meet us according to Tom who has just clicked off the phone, presumably telling Brian we have arrived.

"Meg, I am so sorry. I can't say it enough. I should never have left you alone. I broke my promise, and I will never forgive myself." He holds his head in his hands.

"Tom. *Tom?* Look at me." I tug at his arm until he faces me. "*I* sent you to the doctor. You did the right thing. There is no one who has supported me more on this trip than you. This is not your fault. Hell, you drove all this way with a bad ankle. *I'm* the one that should apologize."

He doesn't answer as Brian is opening my car door. He reaches his whole body inside and grabs me for a tight hug—so tightly that I can't breathe for a moment—but I don't tell him because it's the first time I let go of my tension. And I close my eyes.

Chapter 24

Brian has made a comfy nest for me on his living room couch. I'm surrounded by large pillows and covered with two fleece blankets. He hands me a mug of hot chocolate with so many marshmallows on top that I can't even see any liquid in my mug. "You can go back to the station. I'm really okay."

He wrinkles his forehead and looks at me like I'm crazy. "I'm never letting you out of my sight again—at least until this asshole is arrested."

"You can't be serious. You've only been anchoring for a couple of months. You don't have enough seniority to have earned unlimited time off. No one can harm me when I am locked in your condo. I can't live like a prisoner all day long. Even the FBI agent who talked to me before I left Wisconsin told me I didn't have to live that way. I have to be aware of my surroundings and stick to public places. I've got pepper spray and a whistle. I have a fully charged cellphone. I…"

"And what good did any of that do you in Wisconsin?"

"I was alone in the middle of nowhere. My guard was down. It's not down anymore." I sip the hot chocolate, sure to suck in melted marshmallows.

"I'm taking off tomorrow, too, so I'll be with you until Monday morning, at least. Then we can talk.

I roll my eyes, but I know I am loved.

"Here, I got you a gift." Brian drops a stack of magazines on the coffee table next to me.

I reach out and grab the top magazine. *"Bridal magazines?"* I raise my eyebrows in surprise.

"You need a different type of stress to focus on, so welcome to wedding planning." He smiles like a little boy so proud of having accomplished something new.

"That's actually the first good idea you've had today." I stifle a laugh.

Brian sits on the floor next to the couch and turns to me. He puts his hands on both of my wrists, rubbing them gently. "Meg, I don't know why this is happening to you, but we will figure this out, or the FBI will at least. But you have to let me do *something* or I am going to go crazy."

I kiss Brian on the cheek. "I love you."

"I love you, too."

When Brian has fallen asleep in the easy chair across from the couch, a victim of emotional exhaustion, too, I pull out my iPad to do something I'd been wanting to do ever since Stuart from the library called me. I type Gordan Lamont into the search engine. I read his obituary.

Gordan Lamont, 83, of St. Joseph, Michigan, died of natural causes on November 18. Born to Royce and Nina Lamont, Gordan rose through the ranks in Lamont Industries, the tool manufacturing dynamo founded by his father, to become the CEO and President of the Company, a role he held until his death. Mr. Lamont, carrying on the tradition of his father, contributed to many philanthropic causes in the county including starting the Maria Lamont Cancer Research Center, The Boys and Girls Club of South County, and Harbor Members Golf Tournament that has now grown to include over 200 participants for the weeklong event that has raised over a million dollars for environmental causes.

Gordan is survived by his son Johnny Lamont. Mr. Lamont was preceded in death by his beloved wife Maria and his parents Royce and Nina Lamont.

Donations may be made to the Suicide Prevention Effort in Memory of Sarah Jackson.

I sit up taller on the couch. *Sarah Jackson.* It's the first time I have seen that name associated with Gordan

Lamont since I saw those names on Dad's birth certificate. It can't be a coincidence, can it? If Gordan was my grandfather and Sarah my grandmother, do I deserve to know their story and why they gave my dad up for adoption? Or do I leave it be as nothing will change? Some say information is power, but what power comes from knowing more of my dad's creation story?

A search of the Suicide Prevention Effort in St. Joseph, Michigan, leads to a lovely website with resources for people who struggle with anxiety and depression, hotline numbers to call, places to go, things to read. I am about to close out the site when I skim to the bottom of the page and see a notation for an *about* feature which had not been prominently featured at the top of the page as such things usually are. I click the link.

In March 1961, a young woman walked into Lake Michigan at Silver Beach during the winter and never walked out. While reports vary as to the cause of death, those close to the young woman spoke of her depression and came to believe that she had intentionally drowned herself. Known as the Secret of Silver Beach, hushed rumors fell over the community after the young woman's death. As a result, family members created the Suicide Prevention Effort far ahead of its time to help other families from having to go through such pain and loss and to remove the stigma from the conditions that often lead to such a choice.

"The Secret of Silver Beach," I say aloud, mesmerized by this piece of the puzzle.

"What? Huh? Did you say something, Meg?" Brian says as he startles awake.

"Oh, sorry. I didn't mean to wake you."

"I wasn't sleeping. I was just resting my eyes."

"Uh-huh. Well, that was an awful long rest." I point to the clock.

"7:00? You must be starving!" Brian jumps up from his chair to head to the kitchen to make dinner.

"Wait. I want to show you something." I review my internet searches with him.

"Do you think those are your grandparents—Gordan and Sarah?"

"I would imagine so. It would be an awfully big coincidence to find both of their names connected to the same town with dates that work for my dad's birth to not be the same people as those on the birth certificate. Sarah would have died about three months after Dad's birth."

"It was probably hard for her to have given him up. Does it say how old she was?"

"No."

"Let me see the obituary again." I reopen the website for Brian to read.

"How did you make the connection to Suicide Prevention Effort?" Brian asks with a quizzical look on his face.

"It's the memorial fund request at the bottom of the obit."

"No, it's not." Brian points to the screen. "It says, *Donations may be made to the Maria Lamont Cancer Research Center.*"

"Someone changed it."

Chapter 25

Char rolls out the red carpet for me today as I return to Chicago Midday. Everything that happened to me in Wisconsin and Michigan with the threats and the attempted *murder*—which I still can't get out of my mind—has been kept a secret to the public. The show wrote off the reason for my abrupt end to my trip around the lake as being due to a quick change in the weather. That—and Thanksgiving is this week—so, no one paid any notice.

"You are a sight for sore eyes, Meg Popkin," says Clive as he greets me with a huge hug and a beautiful long-sleeved deep green dress to wear on-set.

"I missed you, too, Clive, and I've gotten used to dressing myself." I laugh. "I've forgotten how nice it is to have someone pick out something new and pretty to wear."

"I've been saving this beauty just for your return. I can't wait to see you sitting back on that set today."

"I appreciate it, though don't blink because I'm just summarizing my trip. I won't be there for long. I'll be back to change after Becca fixes this face. My skin regimen has sorely lacked while on the road. See you in a bit!"

The only way I can describe Becca's mood when she first sees me is pure giddiness. She envelops me with a giant hug. She kisses each of my cheeks. When I sit in her chair, she wraps me with a new cape covered with butterflies, ready for hair and makeup. It feels like Christmas morning.

"You have no idea how much I have missed you," says Becca. "I have *so* much gossip."

"Good! That's exactly what I need right now. I'm tired of talking about myself!" It's clear that Char hasn't told the staff about my stalker though I shudder to even use that word. However, there is a new security presence. A guard stands at the main door, and we'd all been admonished in a management email about keeping all other doors secured and to not allow in unknown visitors. No one seemed to question the email. It's a sad commentary on our world that a directive about increased security at work doesn't make anyone bat an eye.

Becca leans closer to my ear though we are the only people in the room. "Did you hear about Jessalyn?"

"I heard that she collapsed on set. That must have been scary."

"Girl, you have no idea! Trenton sat completely still like his shoes were superglued to the floor. He was useless. Danni had to rush on set to help shield her until we went to commercial. Then the EMT's came. She came to but was groggy and slurring her words. I wonder if she had a stroke. It was frightening. Trenton was a wreck for days after. He stumbled over his words and forgot the names of the people he was interviewing. He was like a zombie going through the motions. Rumors are that he and Jessalyn were a little more than co-hosts, if you know what I mean."

"I figured."

"Yeah, and he was really shaken up. No one knows what happened. I even point blank asked him the last time he was in my chair, and he swore that no one knew what happened to Jessa."

"That's so scary. You know I can't stand that woman, but I'd never wish her harm. And to collapse while live on camera must have been something," I say as I realize that I could likely watch it myself on social media because that kind of thing spreads faster than a wildfire in a dry California summer, but I have no interest in watching another's misfortune, despite Jessa's ambush of my on-air interview after my train attack when she released the video footage from the station's security camera.

"But *everybody* loves your travel segments. They are the highlight of each show. You've seriously been killing it."

"Thanks, Becca," I say as she applies a thick layer of dark eyeshadow to my eyelids. "I enjoyed my trip more than I imagined I would."

Char pops her head around the corner. "Hey, Meg, Becca. Can I borrow you, Meg, when you are done in here?"

"Sure."

"She misses you," Becca whispers when Char is gone. "It's not the same around here without you."

"But I'm sure it's no secret that they are looking for a better fit for Trenton, someone who has better on-air chemistry with him. Jessalyn fits that bill better than me."

"No way. It's gross. She drips with fake compliments for him, but I think there's more competition under the surface than Trenton likes. It seems forced, but in a different way than you and Trenton."

She unravels the curling iron as beautiful ringlets hang on my shoulders. "Thanks, Becca, for the updates. Tomorrow, I want to hear about that new guy in your life, okay?"

"It's a date!" She kisses me on the cheek, and I walk to Char's office. I knock on the door until she calls me inside. I close the door behind me and sit in front of her desk.

"First of all, how are you doing?"

"I'm good. Well, I'm trying to be good. It's been a—*mixed bag*—the last couple of weeks.

Char nods her head. "Yes, I imagine it has been. Here, too, in a different way of course, but nothing has gone quite as planned since the show began. Trenton is a mess. It appears that though your *chemistry* together wasn't conventional, it tested better than he and Jessa, and ever since her abrupt exit from the show, he's seemed, well, *lost*."

"That's too bad," I say though I don't mean it. Trenton is one individual I have difficulty having *any* sympathy for.

"Danni has really been trying, but…"

"Danni?"

"Yes. You didn't know? She's been filling in for Jessalyn since her…uh, accident."

"Oh, that's actually a great idea. She's already used to being on camera with her cooking segments."

"Yes, but Trenton isn't responding well to the transition."

"Char, I know you have a lot of staffing decisions to make—or management does." It's a low blow to Char's real control here, but it's true, and I am sick of hearing about how tough things have been for Trenton when I have been an actual target of *attempted murder*.

Char pauses before answering. "Yes, with that being said…" She clears her throat. "*We'd* like to test you with co-hosts next week while Trenton takes some time off."

If I had been drinking coffee, I would have spit it across Char's desk. This was not the conversation I was expecting. "I don't know what to say. For weeks, I have felt like I was being fired, or at least demoted, and now you tell me that maybe it's *Trenton* who is being replaced? No offense, but our audience is not stupid. They will figure out that Chicago Midday doesn't know up from down. We will be the laughingstock of the city."

"I can let management know that you are not interested then," Char says, reaching for the phone.

I know I've gone too far. Part of me doesn't give a damn, and part of me cares very much. "Wait, Char, I'm sorry. I've been through a lot the last few weeks. I'd be happy to co-host again next week. But, if not with Trenton, then with who?"

"Well, I was hoping you could convince Brian."

Chapter 26

"Absolutely not," Brian says when I approach him at dinner, Thanksgiving leftovers after our small family affair earlier in the week at Rick and Lara's house. Rick spends much of his days sleeping, so we'd only stayed for a couple of hours. It had taken a small argument with Lara to allow me to order the meal from a local restaurant, so no one needed to cook. She'd finally relented when I reminded her that the time together was more important than the food, and we'd all been pleasantly surprised with the tasty choices.

"I was expecting that answer—and I respect it. But Char insisted I ask. I've just been too nervous to bring it up."

"Meg, I have my dream job anchoring the nightly news in a large market. Unlike you, I don't want emotional, thoughtful stories. And, no offense, but I don't want pop culture, either."

"No offense taken."

"I like the hard-hitting news stories."

"I know. And I love that we both know what we want." I rest my hand on Brian's shoulder before taking a large bite of turkey stuffing.

"So, what do you think they will do now?"

"I have no idea, and right now I don't care."

We finish dinner, watch an old James Bond movie, and fall asleep after making love in a nest of disorganized sheets and blankets. It is a blissful night.

There is a voicemail from an unfamiliar number on my phone when I wake up the next morning. I put the phone to my ear and turn away from Brian who is lightly snoring.

This is Van Winkle with the St. Joseph Newspaper. I'd like to speak with you about a story I am writing about Gordan Lamont. Please call me back. The story is under deadline.

Brian turns over and kisses my shoulder. "Are you working on the weekend?" he asks.

"Nope. I got a message from a reporter snooping into my alleged connection with the Lamont family."

"How did the reporter get *that information?*" Brian sits up in bed and runs his hand through his thick hair, a sign of stress.

"That annoying, nosey librarian talked to him. I should never have told him what I was doing."

"Librarians are *supposed* to help with research. Don't beat yourself up."

"Yeah, they're not supposed to *betray* the researcher, though."

"Are you going to call him back?"

"No way."

"Good. You have a big day today."

"Yep! Dress shopping!" I put down my phone, roll over, and kiss my fiancé until I am exhausted again.

After dropping off Brian at Rick and Lara's house, Lara and I drive to Betty's Bridal Boutique. I'm doing this as much for Lara as for myself. She needs a distraction from Rick's upcoming surgery. She's been a basket case, for obvious reasons. And knowing about my *situation* hasn't helped with her stress level. I'd been given strict instructions from Brian, and the FBI for that matter, to watch my surroundings, limit my visibility, etc. I'd asked Lara to drive today after making sure that Brian and I weren't followed to her house just in case whoever is messing with me knows what kind of cars Brian and I drive now. I am finally the proud owner of a car with a fob start. I'd also made an appointment in the private bridal suite with Betty so that no one could observe my dress modeling. She thought my request was because of my local celebrity. If she only knew that was not the real reason at all. Would anyone even want to be around me knowing that I was a target of something I could not fathom?

"What style are we wanting, Ms. Popkin?" asks Betty, a tall, older woman with red hair bound in a fierce bun that pulls her skin back with a sort of natural face-lift effect though she still has a quick small smile.

"I haven't given it a lot of thought…"

"She would look great in anything, Betty, but I'd love to see Meg in something straight that hangs close to her legs, some pretty lace overlay, but classic, not slutty," interrupts Lara who is fingering all the gowns on the racks in the private suite.

"What she said," I say, pointing at Lara.

For the next two hours I forget about stalkers and work drama. And Lara forgets about brain tumors and kid drama. I try on a dress with metal spikes over the bra cup, just for giggles, after trying on several traditional dresses. It's nice to hear Lara laugh again. It reminds me of the preciousness of life, of life's blessings. We drink wine and eat crackers and cheese in between dresses. Being pampered is a lifestyle I could get used to.

I'm beginning to think that I might not find *the dress* today or if there really is such a thing, when I come out of the dressing room to step upon the small stage. I twirl around as I'd done with every other dress, but when I stop to look at myself in the mirror, I know instantly that I've found *it*. The gown features a floral lace overlay with a mermaid shape that hugs my body in all of the right places, yet the high neckline and slight slit in the legs symbolize class.

"Oh, Meg, you are stunning," Lara says as she wipes at the corners of her eyes. "You look like Mom. She'd be so proud of you, both Mom *and* Dad."

"Thank you, Lara." I wipe my own eyes. "I'll take it," I tell Betty.

"Can you imagine someone actually wearing the boob-spiked dress?" Lara chuckles as we drive back toward her house, relaxed and happy.

"The only positive is that no one could hug me! I'm a germaphobe after Covid!"

"That's true," she laughs again.

Lara turns onto her street as I am punching in the number of a pizza restaurant to order dinner for us all before Brian and I go back to the city tonight.

I don't see what she sees, but I feel the car accelerate as she screams, "Oh my God!"

I look up from my phone to see an ambulance parked outside her home. "It's okay, Lara. It's going to be okay." I put my hand on her arm.

She hits the brake, parking the car across the street from her house. I have to turn off the ignition and close her door which she's left wide open on the street.

Brian is on the front porch with the kids wrapped around him, even Blake. Lara is jumping into the back of the ambulance before I even get to Brian.

"What happened?" I ask, glancing down at the boys who all have tears falling down their sweet faces.

"Daddy fall down," says Nolan.

Owen shakes his head. "He was talking and playing with us."

"Then he dropped to the ground," says Blake.

"Uncle Brian call the doctor," says Nolan.

"Paramedics," Owen corrects.

"Paramefic," Nolan repeats.

Owen doesn't correct him.

"Come on, boys. Let's go back inside. It's cold out here." I open the door. Everyone goes in but Blake.

Brian and I look at each other. "I'll get the boys a snack," says Brian, closing the door and leaving Blake and me on the front porch.

"What's going on?" I ask my first-born nephew. He looks so grown-up, almost my height right now.

Blake looks at me with misty eyes, but instead of the young man he is becoming, all I see is the little boy who used to crawl into my arms for story time. I hold out my arms, and he collapses into them. We don't talk. We don't need to.

The younger boys are distracted easily enough with pizza and popcorn and the Teenage Mutant Ninja Turtles Movie. Blake sits in the room and plays Roblox on my iPad. The phone rings an hour and a half later. "It's Lara," I whisper to Brian and move to the bedroom to take the call.

"He's in surgery, Meg." Her voice is quiet but not broken as I'd expected. "They think the tumor is pressing on a blood vessel in his brain, which may have led to his collapse, so they decided to do the brain surgery today. That damn thing is coming out right now."

"That's *good* news, Lara."

"How are the boys?"

I sigh. "They are scared, especially Blake. But they are fine. Don't worry about anything here."

"I don't. Thanks, Meg. I love you."

"I love you, too, Sis. Give us an update."

Nolan has fallen asleep on Brian's chest, and Owen is finishing a puzzle when my phone rings again three hours later. It is much too late for us to have let the boys stay up, but I'm too afraid to send them into a night of possible nightmares. Blake grabs my phone before I do.

"It's Mom. Can I talk first, Aunt Meg?"

"Sure, Blake. Go ahead."

He stands up and takes the phone into the next room, away from his brothers. Life has a way of making you grow up sooner than you were intended to.

Blake is wearing a large grin when he returns. "Mom said the surgery was a success. The doctor got all the tumor. He will need to stay in the hospital a few nights and rest at home for a couple of months, but it's going to get better, Aunt Meg. Dad is going to…live." He whispers the last word, and for the second time today I open my arms for my nephew.

Chapter 27

This message is for Meg Popkin. This is Johnny Lamont. I…uh…I think we might have some things to talk about. Please give me a call. Thanks.

I stare at the transcribed voicemail on my phone. Is there *no one* Stuart the snoopy librarian hasn't given my phone number to? This has to end. I pull out the business card I'd collected from the dining room table at the rental in Bridgman, Michigan, where I'd stayed during my Warren Dunes and St. Joseph tapings. The same couple also own a rental in St. Joseph on Silver Beach. It's time to book the house and address these rumors once and for all and let Mr. Lamont know that I have no intention of interfering with his inheritance.

Chicago Midday couldn't find anyone to replace Trenton on such short notice, so they decided to keep him on for now with Danni and then let Danni and me co-anchor next week. This week I'm doing short pieces, highlighting holiday happenings in and around Chicago. I'm fine with that. I've missed being out in the city more than I thought possible. The only difference is that security hired by the show goes with me everywhere. There have been no more notes and no more *attempted murder* since I've been home. I still can't wrap my head around the whole bizarre thing.

"Meg, can I talk to you for a minute?" Trenton asks as he pops into my office. He's wearing a red sweater and a light layer of camera-ready makeup.

"Choose a seat," I say, waving my hand over my simple, but comfortable set of polka-dotted upholstered chairs.

"Thanks. I'm sorry we haven't really talked much since you returned." He looks down at his shoes.

"To be fair, we didn't talk much before I left except when we had to."

Trenton shrugs his shoulders. "I guess."

I'm not used to this Trenton. He seems a fish out of water, not sure what to say next or how to say it to me when he'd had no trouble being a pompous asshole during most of our relationship. "What do you need to say?"

"I think they're trying to push me out." He balls his hands into fists.

"And what do you think I have thought about my little travel situation? You don't think that *I* feel like *you're* trying to push me out and replace me with Jessalyn?"

"I guess there's some truth in that. But maybe oil and water make for more interesting television than sugar and high fructose corn syrup because that's what it was like with Jessa and me and certainly with Danni. She's the *worst*, Meg."

"Danni? I thought you loved her. We all do."

"She's fine for the cooking segments, but as a co-host she won't let me get a word in, and she fawns all over me—way worse than Jessa. At least Jessa could tell a news story. But then she had her accident or whatever the hell that collapse was. I need a break. I don't want to be fired, though."

"Starting a new show is harder than it looks, huh?"

"It sure is. Anyway, thanks for letting me make my peace. I think things will be—*better*—with you being back." Trenton smiles before getting up to leave.

I speak before I can stop myself from careful thinking. "Brian and I are going to Michigan next weekend. I want to follow up on a story there. We booked Friday and Saturday nights at a rental on Silver Beach, but Brian just found out he's got to cover the Sunday morning broadcast. So, if…uh, if you'd like to come out on Saturday night, maybe the three of us could have dinner, make a fresh start, if you will. And you can have our last night at the rental. Of course, it'd be super great if…"

"If I paid for my night?" Trenton smiles devilishly.

"Well, it'd be nice."

"That actually sounds great. I could use a little road trip. Thanks, Meg. Gotta head out. Danni and I are interviewing the mayor."

"Whoa! That's serious stuff."

"Yeah. Now if I can just get Danni to focus more on him than on me, that'd be great."

"I never thought you could unlearn narcissism." I roll my head back with laughter as he gives me the finger and walks away.

"You did what?" Brians asks as he helps me pack a few more boxes in my apartment in Brookfield, a little bit every week, so we will be ready to move when we can find time to look for a bigger place than either of our current homes.

"I know. I regretted it almost the minute the words flew out of my mouth." I add books from my bookshelf to the donate box.

"I think it's a fantastic idea!"

My eyes widen in surprise. *"Really?"*

"Yeah. It might be exactly what your professional relationship needs to get on track. Good idea, babe." He steals a kiss as I thumb through a stack of old magazines.

"Huh. You are wiser than you look."

He picks me up and deposits me on the bed. I can't stop laughing, even when he removes his pants and mine. If this is what happily ever after looks like, I'm glad I signed up. Now, if only we can nail down a date and a wedding venue.

Chapter 28

"What do you think about a spring wedding?" Brian asks as he unloads the car into our rental in St. Joseph. This time of year, rental availability is plentiful. The fact that we'd been able to find a rental directly on Silver Beach was amazing. Though it's dark and freezing, waking up to a view of the expansive beach and Lake Michigan will be exactly what my frayed nerves need.

"Like *this* spring?" I grab my laptop bag from the backseat.

"Yes. It's December, so a May wedding is totally doable, right? I mean, you already picked out your dress. And Rick will be fully recovered by then. The pathology report came back clean. I'd love for him to be in the wedding party."

"There's a lot more to planning a wedding than having something to wear. And I love that you want Rick to be in the wedding. There is nothing that makes me happier than knowing that my family gets along so well." I punch the code into the lock box—our home away from home, at least for one night.

"Do you think we can get a place in the city, or does that require more advanced planning?"

I shake my head and laugh at my adorable fiancé. "My dear, you are so naive, but I love you."

"Okay, then what about getting married at a park?"

"An outdoor wedding in spring? Have you forgotten that you live in the Midwest? It could be fifty degrees and raining. No way."

"If I didn't know better, I'd think you were trying to delay this wedding."

"Come here, big guy," I say as I grab the front of Brian's Arizona Cardinals sweatshirt, a nod to his home state, and pull him closer to me. "There is nothing you can do that could keep me from marrying you, whether it is tomorrow or in five years. I've been a bit distracted if you recall."

"I know. I'm sorry." He takes a piece of my hair with his finger and tucks it behind my ear. "I'm just ready to wake up to your grouchy morning face and stinky breath every day for the rest of my life."

He runs into the kitchen before I can swat him.

The next morning, though we've barely been here for any time, we pack our bags so we are ready to leave tonight after dinner with Trenton. It's a quick trip, but I need to put the Lamont family story to bed. My father was adopted. It happens. And in the late 1950s and early 1960s, out-of-wedlock births were more scandalous than they are now. Dad had a wonderful family that raised him. I'm sure if he could, he'd thank Gordan Lamont and Sarah Jackson for allowing him to be raised by loving parents. Money never motivated my dad, so the possibility that he'd have been heir to a fortune would not have changed his opinion of how his life turned out. I am sure of it. And it certainly doesn't change mine. I just need to convince Johnny Lamont of that fact.

"Want to leave early and walk around St. Joe before our meeting with Mr. Lamont?" Brian asks as he puts gel in his hair in front of the bathroom mirror.

How did I get so lucky to marry such a handsome creature? "We can do that. Let me grab my sweater and gloves. The wind is always cold off the lake. And I love how you sound like a local calling the town St. Joe."

"Well, you know, the city might be your actual heritage, so I thought that'd give me permission to pretend to be a local."

I laugh. "Makes sense."

First, we walk on Silver Beach along the edge of the lake. It's amazing to think that in a couple of months the water may be frozen chunks of ice. But, for now, the water is lapping gently along the sandy shores, cold to the touch.

"Look!" I bend over and scoop out a rock from the sand and hand it to Brian.

"A heart-shaped rock? That's a good sign." He deposits the rock in his pocket. "Maybe we should get married on Silver Beach. Perhaps a romantic beach wedding?"

"Let's not get crazy."

We walk up the bluff to the downtown area of St. Joe. The stores are still open, surprisingly, though I suppose they are gearing up for Christmas shopping season. I can't believe Christmas is only a few weeks away. The first Thanksgiving without Dad had been odd, but everyone was so worried about Rick that we didn't focus on Dad not being present. However, Christmas was always a special celebration. Mom decorated with not one, but *two* trees, a real tree with white lights and an artificial tree with colored lights There'd be garland on the stair railing, Santa Claus soap dispensers, snowmen floor mats, nativity sets, Advent calendars, and so much more. After Mom died, Dad had tried to carry on the tradition the first year, but nothing looked right, and everything seemed out of place. He couldn't find the stockings. He forgot to buy new ornaments for Lara and me, a tradition since birth, and Baby Jesus was missing from the nativity. Lara had moved the holidays to her house after that, new traditions. Now Dad's gone, too. So much change.

We buy peanut butter fudge at the fudge shop and a Lake Michigan sweatshirt at the souvenir store. Every small town along the lake has shops like these, I noticed on my trip around the lake. I'm not nervous that I'm being watched because no new threats have occurred since I was in Door County. Plus, Brian is with me, so no harm could ever come now. That's how safe I feel with him.

I am in a good mood when we walk into a restaurant in downtown St. Joseph that overlooks Lake Michigan from up high on the bluff. It's cold, thirty degrees, but there are no clouds in the sky, and the sun is shining. The sun shining on a thirty-degree day can fool you into thinking you are on a tropical beach in Florida when you're just staring out a window. And with Silver Beach a hundred feet from our restaurant, I close my eyes and imagine that's exactly where I am. Maybe Brian was on to something about a beach wedding, only I imagine a Caribbean Island setting.

I'd been instructed to ask the hostess to be led to the private party room in the back of Silver Beach Eatery. I guess when your family has infused money all over the town you can claim your own private room at any restaurant.

Johnny Lamont stands up from his table when Brian and I enter the room. He's wearing a sports coat, khaki pants, white shirt, and yellow tie. His hair is gray, and he has a full beard. Though several years younger than Dad, he looks aged. It's the sight of his eyes, though, that cause me to suck in my breath and reach for Brian's hand. He sees it, too, because he squeezes my hand tightly. He has Dad's eyes, deep blue with a twinkle that shines through no matter the amount of light in the room.

"Ms. Popkin," he says, extending his hand. "It's nice to meet you."

"Thank you. Please call me Meg. This is my fiancé, Brian."

"Ah, yes. I've caught some of your newscasts when I've been in Chicago for business," he says, shaking Brian's hand.

"Do you go to Chicago often—for business?"

"At least once a month. I have a place on the Gold Coast with a good view of the lake."

"But you have the best view of the lake right here in St. Joe," I say, pointing out the window of the restaurant to the currently barren beach except for a few seagulls that have remained for the upcoming winter season.

"Silver Beach is most definitely a beauty." He stares off in the distance as if lost in memories of his times spent on the beach, likely many. "Did you know there used to be an amusement park on Silver Beach? Please, have a seat." He points to the leather-covered, high-backed chairs.

"I'd heard that when I was reporting my segments for Chicago Midday. Tell us more about the amusement park, though." I take a drink from a water glass on the table. I notice there is no ice and hope that's not a bad omen.

"My family has connections to the amusement park, you know?"

"I didn't know." I sit quietly waiting for him to continue.

"I don't know if you know much about my family." He pauses and stares at me as if defying me to say *our* family, but I don't dare, nor do I feel a claim to the Lamonts. "My Uncle Albert and a friend built the first boardwalk at Silver Beach in the late 1880s. They started with penny carnival games and grew to add rides. The Sandy Spitfire—a rollercoaster ride that zoomed in the air above the sand—was where I met my wife Heidi." He looks off into the distance again. "We had our first kiss on that ride when our car got stuck in the air for over an hour. She'd been terrified, so I'd protected her, of course." He laughs, a faraway look plastered on his face as if he's reliving the whole evening in his mind. "She hasn't let go since. And I'm grateful. Who knows if she hadn't been forced to sit with me in the air on that day if she'd ever have given me that much time again?"

"That's a beautiful story. What happened to the amusement park?"

"My family sold it to an out-of-state company in the late 80s, and it was never the same again. Lamont Industries became our family's full focus by then, and there's something to be said about a business being run well when the owners have personal investment in the community in which it exists. The new owners of Silver Beach World saw the cash cow that the amusement park was, but they weren't willing to put the money in to continue its profitability by keeping it maintained. So, combining lack of care with a few crime incidents on the boardwalk, and it went to pot."

"Sorry to hear that. It sounds like it was quite the experience back in the day," says Brian.

"It really was. But, about fifteen years ago, my family was instrumental in bringing a carousal back to Silver Beach and created the Silver Beach Historical Museum. Two of the horses on the carousal were restored from the originals that stood right down there," Johnny says, pointing out a window at the beach. "It was very important to my father to leave something positive with our community's history for everyone to enjoy. He always stressed the positives of this beach and what it offers as it isn't…it isn't always a positive experience at the beach for everyone."

"What do you mean?" I ask, wondering if he is thinking of Sarah Jackson's death.

"I guess that's why you are here, right, Meg? You want to know if the Secret of Silver Beach is true? Did twenty-year-old Gordan Lamont impregnate sixteen-year-old Sarah Jackson, force her to give up the bastard baby, and then shun her until she fell into an unrecoverable depression and walked into Lake Michigan to never come out again?"

I suck in my breath and look quizzically at Johnny Lamont. I am taken aback by his boldness and crassness with the story of a human life, not to mention my biological grandmother. "Well, you're laying it all out there, aren't you?"

"I assume that's why you were digging up dirt about my family."

"I was *looking for information* about my father, Mr. Lamont—Johnny. I'm a reporter. I don't *dig for dirt.* You've given me far more information about Sarah Jackson than I'd known. That's quite a sad story."

"It is a sad story, for Sarah Jackson's family, but for the Lamonts it was the best decision for them to get rid of the—to adopt out—the baby. Sarah Jackson was a teenager. My father was not. It would have been a scandal had the rumors been confirmed in public. My grandparents worked very hard to squash the secrets. Money has a powerful way of killing a story."

"And, it seems, killing a young woman." I stare into Johnny Lamont's eyes without blinking, realizing that the twinkle he has doesn't match Dad's eyes at all as there was nothing sinister about Paul Hopkin.

"It had to be done. The Lamonts were building an empire. A scandal like that would have destroyed the trust in our family. And, if you think about it, without that decision to give up—*to adopt out* your father—our family may not have accumulated the wealth we've used to bless this community with."

"Perhaps your dad spent the rest of his life paying for his sins by doing good for the community."

"You could say that."

"Why was the Suicide Prevention Effort memorial removed from Gordan's obituary?" Brian asks, a steel tone in his voice.

"Oh that. Damn, old man wrote his own obit and had a relationship with the funeral home director. I had it removed the moment I saw it. No need dredging up old rumors."

"It obviously meant something to your dad to honor Sarah Jackson."

"Her family was taken care of. Don't worry. Her old man, Leo Jackson, has been a thorn in our side on the board ever since my grandparents made a deal with her family to stay quiet in exchange for a cushy board position and a pension. I think that man's going to live forever."

"Well, I appreciate the history lesson, but why did you want to meet with me?" My patience is thin, my temper flaring. I hate this man. How could he share *any* genetics with my father?

"What's your price?"

"Excuse me?" Brian and I say at the same time. I put my hand on Brian's arm. I've got this. "Do you think I am meeting with you to extort money in order to keep quiet about my father?" My voice rises, and Johnny Lamont has the audacity to put a finger to his mouth to quiet me. A new idea jumps to the forefront of my mind, this conversation swirling with the events of the last week. "Have you been following me?"

"Following you?"

"Yes. You have been, haven't you?"

Johnny's face reddens as he pounds his fist on the table. "What are you talking about?"

"Save yourself the trouble. I don't want your money. I don't want to ever see you again. I wish I never knew of your existence. But be assured, I will be sharing this conversation with the FBI, and you will be punished for what you have done to me. That—you can take to the bank!" I pick up my water glass and douse Mr. Lamont with what remains, not looking behind me as I stomp away.

Chapter 29

I am still shaking when we get back to the rental on the beach. Brian has held my hand the whole way back.

"Do you want to go back to the city now?" Brian asks as he unlocks the front door.

I shake my head no. "I told Trenton we'd have dinner with him. I'm not changing my plans because of that jerk."

"Make that call to the FBI. I'm going to check my work email."

"Do you really think I should call?"

"Think about it, Meg. You didn't get a note on your car until you started researching the Lamont family, and you already told me that the library guy was super gossipy. He probably called Johnny Lamont the minute you went into that research room named after *his* family."

"Maybe, but it still seems like a stretch that he'd chase me or have me chased all around the lake. I still can't believe that I accused him. Why would he have made threats? Just to scare me?"

"Maybe—to scare you into taking his bribe and not sharing the story of your father's birth."

"But he didn't even offer a bribe until today. And why would my dad's birth harm his family *now?* It was over sixty years ago when he was born. Out-of-wedlock sex is not a big deal anymore."

"But statutory rape is still a big deal. Your grandmother was sixteen. He was twenty. The story coming out now would embarrass the family especially after all the accolades Gordan Lamont is receiving. I've read the online posts about him. He is well-revered, clearly *nothing* like his son."

"Attempted murder is a big deal, too. It seems like such a stretch to accuse Johnny of that."

"It's a big stretch to think that *anyone* would do this to you."

"Okay. I guess I'll let the FBI sort it out. I'll make the call."

Brian and I are enjoying margaritas from a mix I'd packed for the trip while waiting for Trenton in the three-season room of the rental, warmed by a portable heater at our feet, when the phone rings. "It's Johnny," I say, glancing at my phone.

"Let me take it," Brian says, reaching for my phone.

"No, thanks," I whisper. "Appreciate it, but I've got it."

Brian nods his head in agreement, returning to his seat across from me.

I click the accept call button on my phone and the speaker button so Brian can hear the call, too. "Hello?"

"Why in the hell did you call the FBI? How dare you?"

I silently count to five. "I gave the FBI information that I told them may or may *not* be useful. I told you I've had several *threats* against me that began after I started learning more about the Lamont family."

"They are sending an FBI agent to interview me at my home. Do you know what that will look like to my neighbors? I live in a *gated community*, Meg. People will talk."

"I am sure the FBI will come in a discreet car. They are only asking questions."

"Do you know who I am?"

"I know exactly who you are, Mr. Lamont, based upon my communications with you. First, you accuse me of trying to extort you for money. Then you yell and scream at me. How am I *not* supposed to think that you might be the one responsible for leaving me threatening messages? And let me tell you one more thing. I can also recognize exactly who you are *not.* You are *not* the man your father was according to what I've read about him. But I can assure you that his other biological son—*my* father—was a kind, generous, and loving man. Seems your father's best genes were all used up when my father was born. Don't contact me again." I click the red button on my phone, drop it on the couch, and take another deep breath. My hand is trembling.

"Holy crap. You went there," Brian says as he looks at me, wide-eyed.

"I guess I did. Pour me another margarita." The doorbell startles us both. *Trenton.* "Don't say anything. I still don't trust him."

"No worries about that."

Chapter 30

Trenton, Brian, and I order Chinese food at a downtown restaurant. I've never spent as much time in any state other than my home state of Illinois until this year in Michigan. It's been both the location of great love, great fear, and great sadness. What a whirlwind year it has been.

"Thanks again for the offer to finish out your rental agreement. I really needed a break."

"I'm glad you were free to take a night. It'd be a shame for such a beautiful place to have gone unused."

Trenton smiles slightly and clears his throat. "So, I talked to Char after you left yesterday," Trenton says in between bites of his chow mein noodles.

"Are you plotting behind my back, Trenton?"

"I'm not plotting anything. I know you don't trust me. I get that. But I'm telling you, after anchoring with kiss-up, camera-hog Jessalyn and smothering Danni, I know what a good thing I had with you, what *the show* had with you." He shudders involuntarily.

"I know what Jessalyn is like, but was Danni *that* bad? She's a chef by trade, of course, but she has good camera presence."

"Meg, she would not leave my side. She'd be at my dressing room door within minutes of my arrival, insisting we review everything we had scheduled for the day. She'd tell Clive what to dress me in so that we matched…"

"I can't imagine Clive taking that direction well."

"He didn't, but Danni kept bugging him until he relented—more than once."

"I did notice some rather cute matching reindeer sweaters," Brian says with a twinkle in his eye.

"Exactly! That never would have happened if Meg had been there."

"I don't agree. Do you not remember our Halloween week of costumes?"

"That was different. It was a holiday revolving around clothing."

"I think you're reading into things. Danni is thrilled for the opportunity to co-host. She may be going a little overboard, but she's only learning from the best, right?" I raise my eyebrows in an *isn't that what you consider yourself* kind of way.

He shakes his head. "There's more," Trenton says almost too quietly to be heard.

"What did you do?" I lean forward though the restaurant is quiet for a Saturday night.

"I may have slept with Jessalyn—and Danni."

"Together?"

"Oh, hell no. I'm not into *that!*"

"Well, that explains everything. She's got a crush on you. I suppose Jessa does, too. You've got to get that thing under control," Brian says, pointing at Trenton's lap.

"I know. Anyway, I can't wait to have *you* back as my co-host."

"Well, *I'm* not sleeping with you."

"Thank the Lord," Trenton says, making the sign of the cross.

"So, what did you discuss with Char?"

"I know she is looking to test *you* with other co-hosts, but she can't find anyone who is willing to commit to a daily show. Thanks, Brian, for turning down the gig."

"My pleasure," says Brian, grinning from ear to ear, his dimples dancing on his face.

"Anyway, she *will* find someone. This is a big market. I asked her if she could give us another chance first. Let you and me anchor all next week, see if we—*I*—can behave. Danni can go back to her cooking segments.

She's not suited to a co-host position. That girl is a nutcase."

"And what did Char have to say about this, uh, second chance?"

"She said she'd think about it, that Danni will co-host with you on Monday, but that she'd talk to management and think about their options.

"I'm open to the idea, but things have to change."

"I'm willing to listen."

I can't help but laugh. Trenton hasn't listened with purpose during all the time I've known him.

"Okay. First, you have to give me on-air respect. You have to *be willing to listen* when I am talking on set to guests, or at least you have to improve your acting skills and *pretend* to listen."

"I can do that. I was a theater kid."

Brian laughs before finishing his beer. I think he is quite enjoying himself. Three men in camouflage clothing have caught his attention at the table in front of us, too. Must be hunting season in Michigan.

"Second, you have to come to me first if you have concerns or suggestions for the show before running to

Char. We need to discuss things and approach her as a united front when we need something."

"But what if you are not around when an idea strikes?"

"Then you write that great idea down and wait until I show up again."

He scrunches his mouth before he bites into a giant crab Rangoon puff. "Is that all?"

"No. One more thing."

"Yes?"

"You have to go to dinner with Brian and me once a month so I can add things to this list as needed."

"Will you pay?" he grins.

"Maybe—some of the time."

"Okay, Meg Popkin, you have a deal." He reaches for my hand to seal the agreement.

"Wait! I thought of another thing!" I say, pulling my hand back.

"Geesh! Is she always this way?" Trenton shoots a look at Brian.

"Don't bring me into your mess." He orders another beer from the waiter.

"Don't call me a victim—about anything—ever again."

"You're no victim. You're scrappy. And I'm sorry."

We finalize the unofficial back-to-work contract with a handshake and the cracking of our fortune cookies.

"Your future is about to be very exciting," I read from my fortune.

"That's a great one," Brian says as he unfolds his fortune. *"Take time to enjoy the simple things, for they are the important things."*

"Well, isn't that sweet," Trenton teases. "My turn. *Give more of yourself to those around you.* Oh, damn. That's not helpful."

Brian and I are still laughing over Trenton's fortune as we walk from the restaurant to my car. Light snow flurries are falling. We'd decided to drive up the bluff tonight rather than walk. After dropping Trenton back at the rental, we'll drive back to the city. Brian has an early call at the news station as the Sunday morning anchor's wife recently had a baby—a little girl. I can't even imagine what that phase of our life might be like. I've seen all the work that Lara and Rick put into raising their boys. I'm not sure I have that much *whatever it is parents have* inside them in me.

"Stop!" Brian yells, throwing his arm out in a straight line halting my forward movement, much like my mom would do when she'd slam on the brakes as a stoplight turned from yellow to red.

"Brian? What…?"

"What's the matter, dude? It's just a piece of paper on the windshield." Trenton reaches for the note before Brian grabs it off the window, directing me back toward the outside of the closest building.

Brian reads the note but doesn't show it to me. "It's another threat. Stay with Meg. Don't let her out of your sight."

"Meg, what's going on?" Trenton looks so confused. I can't blame him. Char had obviously kept her promise and not told him about the real reason my travel segment was cut short.

"It's a long story that I thought was over but clearly isn't."

Brian is yelling at the top of his lungs. *He* is the only crazy man I see on the block. "Hey! Hey! Show your face, you coward. Do you get off on leaving little notes for pretty girls? Show your face. *Johnny? Johnny, are you out there?*"

I reach inside my purse and pull out my phone, calling the FBI. The local police will be here soon, I am assured.

Brian is out of breath when he gets to me. A couple walking back to their car from the restaurant are staring at him.

"Can someone *please* tell me what in the hell is going on?" yells Trenton.

After the local police have taken their report and talked with the assigned FBI agent by phone, the three of us return to the rental as I fill Trenton in on the past few weeks. The wind is howling off the lake as my thoughts slosh around my brain like the water in Lake Michigan. I thought this was over. I thought we were done.

"Why didn't you tell me any of this?" Trenton's concern is real and appreciated.

"And take the chance that you'd call me a victim claiming attention again? No way."

"Damn. That's harsh."

"But true."

Trenton shakes his head in agreement. "Probably so. I was an ass."

"No one is going to argue with that, man," says Brian. "You two stay in the car. I'm going to look around the yard before we grab our bags in the house and get on the road."

"Are you sure you want to stay here overnight?" I ask Trenton.

"To tell you the truth, I'm a bit uneasy. I might grab a hotel room. I imagine the off-season prices are reasonable. Do you have any idea who's doing these things?"

I shrug my shoulders. "I suspect Johnny Lamont or someone he knows might be involved, but I have no proof. This whole thing sucks." I hold my hand over my chest to steady my breathing. My mind is racing. "You were supposed to have a night on Silver Beach, and we were supposed to have a nice visit, but then we met Johnny Lamont who was an ass, and someone is following me, and…"

Brian opens the car door. "The yard looks fine. We can grab our things. Oh, Meg, you're crying."

I wipe away a couple of loose tears as I get out of the car.

"It's okay. You're safe. Everything is going to be okay. I promise."

Brian pulls me in for a hug. I don't even care that I am crying in front of Trenton. Why is this happening? I want my mom. I want my dad. I want Rick to stay healthy. I want life to be simpler. I want…

"Guys! The front door is unlocked. Did you leave it open? *Danni?"*

Brian releases his tight grip on me and runs to the front door. I follow behind, swatting at the tears on my face.

"Danni? What are you doing here?" Trenton's voice strains abnormally, rising in pitch.

It reminds me of when I got trapped in our garage as a child with a wild squirrel. I'd screamed until I went hoarse.

Danni is standing in the living room of our Silver Beach rental. An odd smile is plastered on her face. She's wearing a slip of a white dress with thin straps, not exactly December beach attire in Michigan. In her right hand is a long kitchen knife and not the bread knife we'd used to cut a loaf of bread for toast this morning.

"Surprise! I wanted my visit to be a secret. You are so good at keeping secrets, Trenton. This time I kept a secret!"

Brian pushes me behind him, using his body as a shield.

"Danni, what the hell do you mean? Put down the knife," yells Trenton.

"No, no. This knife is part of my secret."

"What are you talking about?" Brian asks, anger dripping from his voice.

"Danni has a secret! Danni has a secret!" She starts bouncing around the living room like a marionette doll, her eyes glazed over.

Trenton lunges for Danni's arm that is holding the knife but misses. She whirls around and waves it in the air but not at Trenton. She's waving the knife at me.

"Surprise, Meg!"

"I don't understand, Danni," I say as calmly as I can. I try to reach the emergency call button on my phone that is buried deep in my pocket without her seeing, but I can't reach it.

"My brother couldn't finish the job—useless, lazy bum. You know, if a girl wants to get something done, she really has to do it herself, Meg. You should know that—being the independent, successful celebrity that you are. You make your own fame. You get want you want out of life by the amount of effort you are willing to put in." She laughs like an overacting theater performer.

"You?" I try to steady my voice as reality is becoming clear. "*You* left the threatening notes?"

"Well, I left the first one here in St. Joseph. It really is a pretty place, isn't it? But then I had to get back to my Trenton. Right, Trenton, baby? So, I asked my brother to help. He does anything I tell him to do, if only my sweet Trenton would do the same." She reaches her hand out to Trenton. He rebuffs her. "Aw, baby, you're just like the rest of them, aren't' you? Did you really think I wouldn't find out that you slept with Jessalyn? That was naughty, my baby Trenton. Jessalyn paid for her sins. Did you see that beautiful collapse on air, Meg?" she laughs as she turns to look at me. "But now you have to pay for your sins, too, Meg Popkin." She raises the knife in my direction and lunges at me, thrusting her arm straight out from her tiny frame. "Trenton is *my* co-host. Trenton is *my* man. You don't deserve that job. I deserve it. But I don't want to co-host with *you.* What is Char thinking? Trenton, baby, you need to know that you did bad sleeping with Jessa, but I forgive you. I know she tempted you. I know Char tempted you by giving Jessa a shot at the co-hosting job. I'll forgive you. You'll see. In time I will forgive you. But, Meg, you need to leave us alone. You need to stop threatening my position on that set with Trenton. So? Well? This is really quite an easy decision. You need to go. That's easy-peasy, right?"

"You need to calm down, Danni," says Brian.

"THIS ISN'T A TAYLOR SWIFT SONG! THIS IS MY LIFE, *BRIAN!"* she screams.

"Get out of here, Meg," Brian says as he points to the door.

"She won't get far, Prince Brian. I cut the brake line in your car. It's a blasted miracle you made it up the bluff. Oops! That's another secret I let slip. Silly, Danni. Silly, Danni." She slaps herself in the face with her free hand.

Trenton glances at Brian as I step closer to the front door. "Sure, Danni. I'm sorry…baby. I never should have slept with Jessa. It was…it…it was awful. She's nothing like you. Danni, I mean, look at you, Danni. That dress. You look….you are stunning, sweet Danni. Now, put down that knife, okay?" Trenton steps toward Danni.

She is motionless, staring through Trenton at me as I inch toward the door. "Don't move!" she yells at me, raising the knife in a single motion, making contact with Trenton's arm.

"Danni, you dumb bitch! You cut me!" Trenton yells as he grabs his arm, applying pressure.

"Really, baby? Did you just call me a bitch? Na-na-na. That was a mistake." She runs at him with the knife outstretched. Brian rushes forward, tackling her to the couch as if she's a defender on the opposing football team. She doesn't stand a chance with Brian's crushing six-foot-two form and muscles pinning her wrist until Trenton can grab the knife with his free hand.

"Call the police, Meg!" he yells. I pull my phone out of my pocket and dial 911 while Danni thrashes and kicks on the couch. "Don't you dare bite me, or I'll break your jaw!" Brian yells.

I grab a pair of scissors from a kitchen drawer and cut off part of the bedsheet from the bedroom. I wrap the sheet tightly around Trenton's arm while he sits on Danni's legs.

The police arrive within minutes, already understanding the basics of what is happening after the conversation with the FBI an hour ago though none of us saw this coming. None of suspected that we'd been working with a jealous psychopath. The paramedics take Trenton to the hospital for stitches. They take Danni to jail after placing a spit hood over her head as she acted like a rabid animal spitting at everyone within reach. An officer stays behind to take photographs of the crime scene and to get our statements.

It's nearly midnight when the house is empty except for Brian and me. I feel like a zombie in the middle of a horror movie, lost and sad.

"Come here." Brian pulls me closer. I rest my head on his chest. I don't cry. I'm too in shock to release my emotions. "There are a lot of secrets in this place," he whispers against my ear.

"Maybe we *should* get married at Silver Beach."

Brian pulls away from me. "Are you serious?"

I shrug my shoulders. "My father was born here. He's one of the best things that ever happened in this world. Bookending this crazy madness with another joyous event here might be exactly what is meant to happen."

"You are crazy."

"I know—but good crazy."

"Yeash, I've had enough bad crazy to last a lifetime."

"Understatement of the night."

Chapter 31

"You look beautiful, Meg," says Lara as she smooths out the veil that sits upon my head. It reaches to the ground and will skim the beach as I walk with Tom to Brian. He'd been the logical choice to walk me down the aisle, and I know Dad and Mom are with me in spirit.

"Thanks, Lara. You look radiant, too. Rick is a lucky man." I kiss her cheek, careful not to smudge my lipstick.

"*I'm* the lucky one that Rick is here and healthy."

"We all are. How did you get the boys into their suits?" I look fondly at my nephews who are sitting in the front row awaiting the *big show* as Blake keeps calling our wedding ceremony.

"That was all Rick's responsibility. I am purely focused on you today. I imagine, though, that there were a lot of bribes involved."

I smile. "I imagine so." I look out over the guests that await my arrival on Silver Beach. Johnny Lamont sits in the third row, bride's side. I'd called to apologize for blaming him for being a stalker, but he'd said he understood my reaction when Danni's story broke in the news. It had made the national news, too. *Local Chicago*

News Celebrities Become Victims of Stalker. Trenton was pleased he'd gotten a write-up as a victim, too. Chicago Midday has thrived ever since we returned to co-hosting, in part to the stalking story and in part to our renewed chemistry.

I'd cashed in on the only thing I wanted from Johnny Lamont, a way to host my dream wedding at Silver Beach. He'd pulled some strings with the city council to allow a Thursday night wedding on the beach and a reception to follow at the pavilion that houses the carousel. Weekend weddings in May, June, and July have been full for a year. He'd also mailed me a picture of his father with young Sarah Jackson, the only picture I'd seen of the teenage girl. She glowed in the picture as she looked into Gordan's eyes. They were sitting in the sand and holding hands. *He really did love her,* the message in the card from Johnny had said. *And I'm sorry I misunderstood your motives.*

Jessalyn is sitting with Char, Becca, and Clive. She'd returned to anchoring the news at WDOU's competitor station. Detectives had theorized that Danni had put something in Jessa's food that she ate in the cooking segment right before her on-air collapse. Danni's trial for my attack at Silver Beach is at the end of July. The FBI had discovered that she'd been in and out of mental institutions since she was 14, having changed her name and biography many times over the years. It's sad that *Jeanie Demetrius* never got the help she deserved.

"Ready?" Tom asks, as he enters the bridal suite. "The wedding coordinator says it's go time."

"I'm ready." With a final kiss from my sister, who walks ahead of me down the aisle with Rick at her side, I smile at Tom.

"You look beautiful, Meg."

"Thank you, Tom. Thank you for everything you and Anita have done for me."

"I'm honored that you asked me to walk you down the aisle on this special day."

"There is no one else I'd have wanted except for Dad. But he's here. I feel him."

"He is, Meg. He is."

I lock my arm through Tom's as the wedding march plays.

Brian stands under a pergola at the end of the sand aisle with Lake Michigan at his back and the wind gently rustling his hair. The dimples on Brian's face accentuate the smile that grows as he sees me. We lock eyes until I am standing next to him. "You look ridiculously gorgeous," he whispers as we stand before Anita, who, it turns out, knows how to officiate weddings. That woman never ceases to amaze me.

"Ready for this?" I whisper back.

"Ready and willing." He winks at me.

Life is complicated and weird. Sweet and salty. But sometimes everything comes together on one perfect day when everything you've ever gone through and every moment you've lived makes sense, at least for *this* moment in time.

War and Me By: Marcy Blesy

Amazon Reviewer: *The story and characters draw you in. I felt like I was in the story and feeling the emotions of each character. I laughed. I cried. I couldn't put the book down! The story takes place during the WW2 era and intertwines love with the realities of war. A must read!*

Flying model airplanes isn't cool, not for fifteen-year-old girls in the 1940's. No one understands Julianna's love of flying model airplanes but her dad. When he leaves to fly bomber planes in Europe forcing Julianna to deal with her mother's growing depression alone, she feels abandoned until she meets Ben, the new boy in town. But when he signs up for the war, too, she has to consider whether letting her first love drift away would be far easier than waiting for the next casualties.

War and Me

1943

Chapter 1

It's funny the things you do when you're paired against an adversary called *War*. The thought of collecting other people's junk a few years ago would have disgusted me. But if hunting for scrap metal to turn into weapons to defeat America's enemies would bring Dad home sooner, then I'd do it.

"Julianna, let's get down to the river," said Caroline. "Hurry! No way that boy's getting dibs on the scrap metal out there."

I couldn't stop staring at the unfamiliar boy across the river. He wasn't from Bridgmont. I was sure.

"Maybe we should walk down river a bit. I don't want to look like we're taking over his territory," I said.

"No way. We go upriver. Anything washing downriver he'll have first chance at. We're winning this contest. I need that money for a real dinner," said Caroline. "One night without rations."

We grabbed our boxes and headed upriver. I turned around and watched the lean, lanky boy looking at us. It was real quick, just saw his eyes darting our direction. I couldn't get a good look at his face, but something told me he was none too happy with our decision.

Caroline and I staked out a clear spot along the river. I rolled up my jeans to wade in the water. It was the only pair I owned, and it hadn't been an easy battle to win. I was never a prissy girl wearing bows in my hair or rouge on my cheeks, but convincing Mother had taken work.

"Let's look for long sticks," I said. When I turned around Caroline was already gone, traipsing through the woods like the tomboy she was, indifferent to the snapped twigs and broken logs in her way. She came back with two sticks before I even climbed over my first obstacle.

"Here. This will be perfect." She thrust a stick in my hand. "Just start poking around. Tomkin's is only a half mile up the road, and they put their trash out back. There's bound to be some tin cans washed down the river. I doubt those teenage boys he has working for him are as careful as he'd like. *You know how irresponsible we kids are*!" Caroline burst out laughing at her imitation of her mother.

Caroline often clashed with her mother. She always told Caroline what to do. *"Stand up straight. Make your bed. Wash the dishes. Clean those fingernails."* And she always ended by saying, *"Kids are just so irresponsible these days! When I was a girl..."*

At least her mother cared. She wasn't friendly, but she usually knew what Caroline was doing. My mother had no idea what my day looked like because she didn't ask. It was enough for her to just get out of bed. She didn't smile much. I tried to do everything I could to keep her content, if not happy. Nothing could make her happy with Dad gone.

Caroline and I worked for nearly a half hour finding twenty assorted soup, coffee, and vegetable tin cans. The mosquitoes feasted while we searched, and the humidity flattened my hair. Why I'd even bothered to use curlers this morning was beyond me. My hair always did best when left limp and straight. When I spotted an old bumper sticking out of the water halfway across the river, I felt like my luck had finally turned.

"Caroline! Look!" I didn't wait for a reply. Stepping out on the large, jagged rocks that lined the shore of Hidden River, all I could think about was how we were sure to win the scrap metal competition at our high school if I could get that bumper out. Most kids would only bring in old cans or discarded tools.

As I stepped out onto the third rock, I felt my confidence growing, and I began to imagine myself eating a big dinner down at Hannigan's Diner with my scrap metal earnings. While salivating with thoughts of buttered potatoes and juicy steak, I swatted at a swarm of gnats that were attracted to the water lilies growing on the water's surface. Before I could stop myself, I lost my footing on a slippery rock and landed in the cool river. I must have hit my head on a rock because the next thing I remember I was coming to in the arms of that strange boy from across the river.

Lanky Boy brushed my long hair out of my eyes and yelled at me.

"What are you doing?" I asked.

"Oh, good. You're awake."

"What are you doing?" I asked again as he carried me along the river's bank.

"I'm trying to make sure you're okay is what I'm doing." I reached up to touch my head, wincing at the throbbing pain. My hand was covered in blood. I felt like I was going to be sick.

"Julianna! Your head! We have to get you home," said Caroline, rushing over to my side. "What the hell are you doing?" She turned her attention to Lanky Boy.

"Seems that this is the question of the day. Just looking for a place to put your friend." He dripped water on my face, his hair plastered to his forehead. Staring at his brown eyes was the only thing that kept me from throwing up. Kinda like a milky chocolate bar, the kind Dad used to bring home sometimes after work before he left for war.

"Well, thanks for your help and all," said Caroline defensively, "But how could you have gotten here so quickly? You were downriver the last time we saw you. Are you following us?" She tossed her fiery colored hair behind her back and stuck out her chest. I guess Lanky Boy didn't like her tone because he deposited me on the ground, a bit too hard for my liking.

"Yeah, I guess you could say I was following you. Seems to me you're trying to steal all my tin cans, and that is not rightly fair. This is my territory, and I was here first."

"Well, let me tell you something, Mister!" Caroline fought back. "I don't see any name on this land, so it's free for all. You go to hell!"

"I think I need to go home now," I said. I didn't think a gash in my head would cause a battle in our sleepy little town, but now that it had, I just wanted peace.

"Hold this on your head until you get home," he said. "You'll be fine. The head bleeds a lot." He pulled off his shirt exposing his lean build. He paused only long enough for me to press the cool, wet shirt against my head. Lanky Boy was gone before I had a chance to thank him.

"Let's get you home. We'll take it slow," said Caroline.

I held Lanky Boy's shirt against my head which had stopped bleeding and leaned against Caroline's shoulder as we walked away from the river.

"I feel so foolish," I said.

"Hey, just think if you had managed to pull that bumper out. We'd be hard to beat for sure. That $15 first prize would definitely have our names on it. And how proud our dads would be to know that their daughters collected the most scrap metal."

"Have you ever seen him before?" I asked.

"Are you still thinking about that boy?"

"Just wondering if you've seen him around."

"No. He's not from around here. No local boy is going to ignore some fine beauties like us."

I laughed.

Caroline stopped, defensive.

"Why are you laughing? You laughing at me, Julianna Taylor?"

"You just make me laugh, Caroline. *In a good way.*" Caroline played by her own rules, but I admired her for that. And she was the only one I confided in about Dad.

"Dear heavens! What happened to you, Julianna?" asked Mrs. Hermann when we arrived at Caroline's home.

"I took a little tumble, Ma'am."

"And you're wet!"

"I got a little too close to the river."

"Caroline, get the peroxide."

Caroline did as she was told. Her mother was the only person who could ever make Caroline obey.

Mrs. Hermann examined my head. It still hurt, but there was no more bleeding. The peroxide was another story. I think being stung by a hive of bees would have hurt less than the sting of that peroxide on my head wound. I had to bite down on Lanky Boy's shirt just to keep from screaming.

"No stitches necessary. Why were you girls so close to the water? You need to be more responsible."

I could see Caroline rolling her eyes behind her mother.

"We were digging around for the scrap metal competition, Ma'am. I guess I wasn't too careful."

"Do be more sensible next time." She sighed. Did you collect anything good?"

"We collected a bunch of cans. I'm sure there's a lot more out there, too," said Caroline.

"You should go back and get your collection," said Mrs. Hermann.

"That would be nice, but you won't believe what happene…"

"NO!"

Caroline and her mother stared at me.

"I mean, no, there's really not that much there. It's not worth the trek back to the river. I'm sure someone else will find the cans anyway. I'd really like to go home now."

"Fine. I'll drive you home," said Mrs. Hermann.

"NO!"

"I mean, no thank you, Mrs. Hermann. We don't get too many warm fall days. I'd like to walk…with Caroline…if you don't mind."

"Be practical, dear. It might be diffic…"

"It's fine, Mama. I'll go with her. She's feeling better. I can tell, but she's right. She should get home."

"Then you best get going. Your mother will be wondering why you've been gone so long."

I really doubted that.

The scenery on my mile walk home complimented my mood. I really hated early fall. I knew winter was coming. Soon there'd be less daylight hours, and the snow would come. All the changes just reminded me more of Dad. I wondered what changes he was seeing. Where was he? Where did President Roosevelt send my dad? I'd heard that American troops had landed in Italy. Was Dad there?

"Thanks," I said when we arrived in my yard.

"For what?"

"For not telling your mother about the boy."

"It's fine, really. I don't need her hassles or nagging anyway. But what's the big deal?"

"I don't know. I just don't want her to tell my mother."

"About a boy that was obnoxiously rude? Why does it matter?"

"I don't really know. I just don't want her to know. I can't really explain it,

Caroline." And I couldn't. I couldn't even explain it to myself. The memory of being picked up by the stranger with the brown eyes who'd come to rescue me wasn't something I could shake, and I didn't want to diminish it by talking about it.

"Should I come in?" asked Caroline.

"No sense. Mother's not in much of a mood for company. Thanks."

"Sure thing. And you might want to throw out that bloody shirt," she said gesturing to Lanky Boy's shirt which I still gripped. "It might concern your mother."

"You're probably right. See you soon."

I waved good-bye and tossed the stranger's shirt in the outdoor trash. I doubted Mother would even be awake to notice, but no sense taking any chances. She didn't need any more worries.

Mother was resting, as I'd assumed. It was her favorite past-time lately. I rinsed my long hair in the bathroom sink. I closed my eyes while the blood ran down the drain, wishing I could wash away all my worries as easily. When I finished, I examined myself in the mirror. My brown hair came from my dad, but my green eyes came from my mother, and sometimes, when I didn't have enough sleep, they had a hollow appearance, too. I always tried to get enough sleep. I opened the bathroom door. Mother stood at the top of the stairs, her hair stiff and ratty, pulling loose from her bun. The dark circles under her eyes told *her* story. It was my story, too. We shared the same story, but her pages were stained by tears. She couldn't see the happy ending I hoped for.

We both heard the mail fall.

The Secret of Blue Lake (1)

The only true certainty in life is dying, but there's a whole lot of life to live from beginning to end if you're lucky. When Chicago news reporter Meg Popkin's dad makes a surprise move to a tiny town called Blue Lake, Michigan, in the middle of nowhere and away from his family after losing his wife to cancer, she wonders if there is more to the move than *just a change of scenery*. With the help of a new, self-confident reporter at the station, Brian Welter, she tries to figure out what the secret attraction to Blue Lake is for its many new residents and along the way discovers that maybe she's been missing out on some of the joys of living herself.

Drama, mystery, and romance abound for Meg as she learns about love, loss, and herself.

The Secret of Silver Beach (2)

After solving the mystery of the secret of Blue Lake, Meg returns to Chicago and to her new job as co-host on Chicago Midday. But when poor chemistry with Trenton

Dealy leads to problems on the show, Meg is assigned a travel segment that will send her on location all around Lake Michigan visiting beach towns and local tourist attractions. The trip takes her away from fiancé Brian who has to continue anchoring the nightly news in Chicago. When odd threats start hurtling in Meg's direction, she finally confesses to Brian and those closest to her that she might have a stalker. Do the threats have something to do with the new information she learned about her dad's past in the little town of St. Joseph, Michigan, or is there something bigger at play that threatens more than Meg's livelihood?

Marcy Blesy is the author of over thirty children and young adult books including the popular series, EVIE AND THE VOLUNTEERS, NILES AND BRADFORD, THIRD GRADE OUTSIDER, HAZEL, THE CLINIC CAT, and BE THE VET. Her picture book, Am I Like My Daddy?, helps children who experienced the loss of a parent when they were much younger. She has also been published in two Chicken Soup for the Soul books as well as various newspapers and magazines. By day she teaches creative writing to wonderful students around the world.

Marcy is a believer in love and enjoys nothing more than making her readers feel a book more than simply reading it.

I would like to extend a heartfelt thanks to Betty for being the first person to read The Secret of Silver Beach and for giving me her guidance and expertise as my editor. Thank you to Heather, Keri, and Cindy for being fantastic, encouraging readers of an early draft of this book. I am quite fortunate to have trusted and wise friends who continue this journey with me.

Thank you to Ed, Connor, and Luke for always championing my dreams.

Made in the USA
Monee, IL
08 August 2023